WALNUT BROWNIES AND MURDER

A TEMPERANCE MATTHEWS COZY MYSTERY

LITTLE BAKERY COZY MYSTERY SERIES
BOOK 3

LUCINDA RACE

MC TWO PRESS

Editor N.N Light/ Purple Pen Wordsmithing
Cover design by Jacobs Ink LLC

Manufactured in the United States of America
First Edition April 2026

Print Edition ISBN 978-1-966424-51-2
Large Print ISBN 978-1-966424-52-9
Hardcover ISBN 978-1-966424-45-1
E-book ISBN 978-1-966424-53-6

1

───────

I scooped lemon bar batter into the baking pan, carefully swirling lemon zest ribbons across the top. The soft launch of the Early Rise 2.O took place this weekend, and the engagement party for a local couple needed to be a smashing success. No pressure at all.

The kitchen door banged shut. Looking up, I saw my best friend, Josie Shaw, walk in and flopped on a stool with a theatrical groan. She ran a hand through her currently blonde hair, brushing it back from her gray eyes. "I'm exhausted."

With a quick glance her way, my brow arched. "Hello to you, too." I pointed to the coffee pot. "Need some go-go juice?"

"Nah." Josie exhaled and dropped her head to the counter. "If I drink another drop, I'll never sleep tonight. I've hit the twitchy-eye stage of caffeine overload." She lifted her head. "Whatcha baking?"

"Right now? Lemon bars. I've completed the tiny cheese-cakes, petit fours, and mini tarts. After these, the frosted double-fudge brownies with walnuts will round out the dessert trays."

"And this is for the Carmichael-Posey party?" She wrinkled her nose as if those names were distasteful.

"That's right," I slide the pans into the convection oven and set a timer on my phone. "Why the sour face?"

"I'm not sure how it's been for you to deal with them, but after I got the invitations finalized and at the printers," she threw up her hands, "Wendy Carmichael changed them. Again. And now she wants the Posey crest to be incorporated into the design."

I washed my hands and turned, giving her my full attention. "There's a Posey family crest? I thought they were just a normal, wealthy family."

"Right?" She slapped her hand on the countertop. "Apparently, the Posey family claimed the crest in the 1700s before they left Hampshire, England with nothing but a trunk of linens and silver."

"Are they descendants of nobility?"

"I doubt it's historically factual. Something like that would have come out by now on the Oak Hollow grapevine. Honestly, it's Wendy putting on like she's Lady Posey or something." She tipped back her head and pressed her fingertips to her eyelids. "She's the client, so I'll redo the darn invites for a third time, but what a waste of time and money."

"As long as you get paid, that's the upside."

She shot me a knowing grin. "Yeah, that's one way to look at it. How's Wendy been with you? Frosting on a cupcake or vinegar and salt?"

With a laugh, I said, "A cupcake with vinegar frosting."

She laughed. "Upside for you, Temperance—the Oak Hollow Hideaway Inn might become a regular customer."

I crossed my fingers and looked at the ceiling. "From your lips…"

She leaned over the counter and ran her finger over the inside of the bowl, scooped up lemon batter, and licked her finger clean. "This is so good. Any chance you'll have an extra lemon square, brownie or three?"

Bobbing my head to the hand-wash sink, I chuckled. "If you help, you can take a plate home with you."

WOOF. Hank's bark carried from the other side of the door leading from the kitchen to my home. "Sounds like my fur baby needs a break." Tossing the towel from my shoulder to the workbench, I crossed the room.

My hand hovered over the doorknob.

Josie joined me. "I've said it every day for the last two weeks: this kitchen is awesome. Not only did Russ do a fantastic job, but he finished in record time."

"It's pretty great." I glanced at the gleaming stainless steel counters, the bank of ovens against the back wall, the four-burner range next to the sink and dishwasher, and shelves on every open wall space. "The layout is perfect. Baking in here has been better than the brick-and-mortar storefront that burned down." I gave an involuntary shudder when I thought of the fire that changed the course of more than just my life but also the lives of three others.

Josie touched my arm. "It was a tragedy, but you have a fresh start."

"True, but there are events I wish had turned out differently." When I pushed the door open, Hank, my black and tan dachshund, was waiting patiently. His head tipped from one side to the other as he barked again. I scooped him up.

"Hank, you're a good boy." I kissed the top of his head and checked his water and kibble bowls; both were full. Josie slid open the glass door, and he wriggled to get down.

We followed him outside. He pranced around the grass, his nose twitching as he inspected every inch as if he'd never been outside before. I chuckled. "Hank, do your business."

He ignored me. "We might as well sit, and you can tell me how you're going to incorporate the Posey crest into the invitation."

Josie perched on the top step, and I settled next to her.

She said, "It's going to be straightforward. I'll add it to the center top and have it on the return address flap on the back of the envelope."

"What's it look like?" I pulled the ponytail holder from my hair and rubbed the back of my head.

Withdrawing her cell, she tapped a few keys, then handed it to me. "Blow it up. It's actually kind of cool."

I zoomed in as she suggested. "It's a coat of arms, not a crest. See the four quadrants?" I held the phone up for Josie.

"The top left is a blooming rose bush, probably to signify the family name, Posey. The top right is a key crossed with a feather quill." Pausing, I tried to remember what they symbolized. "The key is for hidden knowledge and the quill represents the legacy."

Josie peered closer as I talked. "The bottom left is a ship. That must represent their journey to America."

"What about the last quadrant, the tree stump with the new leaf coming from it?"

I narrowed my eyes and peered closer. "A new beginning, but look just above the symbol. There's a book sealed with a single rose in the wax. *Veritas sub rosa.*"

Her voice was filled with awe. "Is that Latin?"

I tilted my head toward her as I handed over the phone. "Yes, it means *truth beneath the rose.*"

"How mysterious," she whispered as she scrolled over the image. "Do you think there is a hidden meaning?"

"It's hard to say. However, the name Posey is associated with flowers. Maybe the book also represents knowledge. Without searching it and the family history, I can't pinpoint the exact meaning."

"It will add a nice touch to the invite, but I wish Wendy had asked for it before the printers had done the run."

I gave her a shoulder bump. "It'll work out. I'm surprised she hasn't asked me to create a stencil and design a cake."

Josie guffawed. "Give the bride-to-be a moment. It's not every day you get to micromanage the world wearing white silk."

I slapped my hands together and threw back my head in laughter. Hank stopped, stared at me, and then barked before racing to my side. My little sidekick never wanted to miss out on the fun.

I rubbed his velvety ears. "Hank, don't you think Josie's clever?" He barked and wagged his tail as if he agreed.

My phone vibrated as the timer went off. "I need to check the lemon bars." Carrying Hank inside, I closed the door and set him on his bed. "You be a good boy; I'm going back to work."

He lay his head on the blankets, with sorrowful brown eyes, he looked as if he had just been denied cheese.

"You'll be fine," I reassured him.

Josie opened the adjoining door, and the moment we stepped inside, the aroma of citrus and sugar filled the air. I quickly washed and dried my hands before slipping into silicone oven mitts. "Golden yellow and perfectly set," I said as I pulled the cake tester from the center. "A dusting of confectionery sugar and these will cool."

Josie tied an apron on and washed her hands. "Ready, chef."

"Hardly a chef, just a simple baker." However, her comment made me smile.

"What can I do?" she asked.

"The brownie recipe is on the next page. Would you start to gather the ingredients?"

"Of course. How many dozen do you need?"

"Eight, so we need to quadruple the recipe."

"Aunt Lottie's Double Fudge Brownies." She gave me a side glance. "This recipe isn't from your aunt Penny?"

"No, it was my great aunt's on Penny's side. It's the best

brownie recipe I've ever had, and brownies are my weakness."

"Did Wendy indicate this was a nut-less event?"

"She said there were zero allergies and to bake all my treats as I normally would. "My cell rang. I pressed the speaker button. "Hello, 2.O. This is Temperance."

"Thank heavens you answered. Temperance. This is Wendy Carmichael, and I need your help. Would it be possible to drop everything, go to Andrew's parents' house, and pick up platters for tomorrow? I just spoke with Eunice Moss at the inn. She doesn't have enough to display your tiny dessert station. I just don't know what I'm going to do. I still have to get my nails done, pick up my dress from the cleaners, and, well, there aren't enough hours left in today to get it all done. Are you still there, or did you hang up on me?"

I winked at Josie. "Wendy, I was waiting for you to take a breath. So why don't you take ten seconds and do four or five deep breaths?"

"There's no time. Will you help me or not?" Hysteria tinged her words, and I flicked off the ovens.

"Of course. Josie's here, and she can drive out with me, and we'll drop them at the inn. Is there anything else you need?"

Her next words came out in a rush. "You'll do it?"

Calmly, I said, "We're happy to help. Is there anything we should check on at the inn, since we'll be there?"

"Just make sure the desserts will have a nice display. But you're not taking them over today, you'll still deliver tomorrow?"

"I will be at the inn by eleven."

"Make it ten. Just to give yourself plenty of time."

I smiled, hoping it would be evident in my tone. "Wendy, this is a special time for you and Andrew. Your event planner should be dealing with the last minute details, not you."

"I know, but currently he's at another gig and I'm trying to relax, but it's hard."

I heard her fingers snap. "One last favor? Remind my future mother-in-law that she needs to bring the painting of the family crest. I'd like that hung over the buffet table."

Josie mouthed, *Why?*

"That's sweet that you're incorporating the crest into the invitations, too. But I'm confused. Isn't the buffet table outside under the tent?"

"Minor details. It's important for people to know the Posey family is growing and will remain a significant part of this community. I have big plans once Andrew and I are married."

Josie threw her arms wide. I could almost hear her say, *See what I mean?*

"I'll pass the message along. I need to tidy the kitchen and we'll head over."

"Thank you, Temperance. Andrew was right when he suggested calling you for help. If there is any question about the platters, give me a ring. I'll be on my mobile."

She disconnected, and I grinned. "Mobile? Who even says that anymore? That expression's like from a decade or more ago."

"What did I tell you? A bridezilla of the worst kind. Not only is she firing off orders to us, but I can't even begin to imagine her dealing with anyone who's on site tomorrow."

I held my hand up. "I'll be there. She asked. I said I'd help keep the buffet filled. It's only for a couple of hours. Also, I plan to have stacks of business cards in my apron in case someone asks about my petit desserts."

Josie shook her head and laughed. "Did you have to make the engagement party cake too?"

"No, thank heavens. She wanted something similar to her wedding cake, so the event planner is in charge."

Since my bakery was destroyed, I had stopped taking orders for fancy cakes. If I continued with my little bakery, I wouldn't ever go back to the cake business. Besides, brides were temperamental, and delivering works of art in cake form was nerve-wracking.

Josie stashed the flat of eggs in the refrigerator. "Can we leave the dry goods on the counter?"

"Yeah. I'll grab my keys and meet you outside."

I jogged to the front door, locked up, checked on Hank, who was snoozing, and left through the commercial kitchen. Josie was standing next to my SUV.

"Did you bring extra business cards?"

I patted my shoulder bag. "Never leave home without them. I should have asked; do you have time to ride with me?"

"Yeah, it won't take more than an hour or so to redesign the invites. Besides, Eunice was sprucing up the porch and the gardens for this party and I want to see the result."

I laughed and got into the driver's seat. Josie buckled her seat belt and smiled. "Wendy asked her to create a tidier space for the event."

After I was driving up the street, I glanced at her. "She's bold. I'm sure it was lovely already."

"It was." She added the address to my GPS for the Posey house and the second stop for the inn. "Like my grandmother used to say: She's bold as brass."

It wasn't long before we reached the Posey's blacktopped driveway. It was lined with maple trees, interspersed with sections of split-rail fence draped with climbing roses.

"Impressive," I murmured.

Josie grinned. "Wait. You haven't seen anything yet."

The driveway curved gently, and around each bend, a surprise was revealed. On the left, a small orchard—trees heavy with ripening fruit. To the right, a pristine tennis court, an Olympic-sized pool, and beyond them a row of immaculate horse stables marking the entrance to an oversized paddock.

I gave a low whistle. "We haven't seen the house yet."

"You will." Josie pointed out my side of the car.

Just over the hill, peaks of a roofline grew larger. "Do they live in a castle?"

She laughed. "Not quite. It's a family compound. There are wings for each adult member of the family. I've heard that after the wedding, Andrew and Wendy will move in. His mother has had an entire section of the house renovated for them."

"That's quite a wedding present—and no mortgage to start a marriage. Even better."

We turned left and the brick-and-board façade of the house rose in front of us, all three magnificent stories. A wide porch graced the front, I couldn't see if it extended down the side. Luxurious flower pots spilled over with a riot of colors and trailing ivy. I sucked in a breath. "This is spectacular and it's been in Oak Hollow for how many decades?"

"Try centuries. According to the historical society, the original structure was built in the late eighteenth century when the family arrived from England. Apparently, expanding its footprint has been a family hobby ever since. Andrew's mother, Cissy, is an avid horsewoman and added the stables when she married Andrew's dad."

I parked and peered out the windshield, gazing at the Posey family home. "I can understand why Wendy is putting on airs, but her family is wealthy, too."

"Nothing like this. Mr. Carmichael is self-made; there's no generational wealth there. He's a lawyer and now a judge, and his wife is vice president at Oak Hollow Bank, and it's rumored she'll become president in the next few years."

The front door opened. An older woman with short, chicly

styled hair, in slacks and a blouse, crossed the porch and waved.

Josie said, "That's Cissy Posey. Andrew's mother."

I rubbed my hands together. "Let's get the platters, and I have to ask her about that painting for Wendy, too."

2

"Hello there!" Cissy Posey waved and ran lightly down the front steps, reaching us before I closed the door.

"Hi Cissy, it's good to see you again," Josie said.

"Josie, hello. This is a treat. Wendy said you'd be stopping by." She made a beeline for me with her hand extended. "Cassandra Grayson Posey, but everyone calls me Cissy, and you're Temperance Matthews, the talented baker. My husband loved stopping at your bakery during his lunch hour to pick up bread. It's such a shame about what happened."

"That's me. Thank you for your kind words. Tell your husband I'm opening a little bakery from a new commercial kitchen, so I'll be back in the bread business soon."

Her smile widened. "Rob will be thrilled to hear the news. I'm happy that you're making the petit dessert trays for the party. Some of the food Wendy has selected isn't exactly delicious finger foods." She said, "Come inside."

I was curious about that statement as we followed her up the brick path into the house. Entering the front hall felt like stepping into the lobby of a five-star boutique hotel. Although grand, it kept its cozy feel, complete with a painting of a family crest hanging on the opposite wall. Surely that wasn't the painting Wendy wanted at the party.

"Your home is lovely." I couldn't help but marvel as my gaze swept the space. Gilded frames graced old oil paintings against the off-white walls. A crystal chandelier hung from the third floor, casting soft lighting over the open staircase. At the base of the stairs was an upholstered bench with mahogany claw feet next to a marble table. The polished wood floors gleamed around the edges of an enormous floral rug that tied the space together with timeless elegance.

"Thank you." Cissy paused in a doorway and took in the space. She had a distant look in her eyes. "As a young bride, it took me a while to get used to the size of the home when I moved in. I was lucky that my late mother-in-law was welcoming, and within a few months, she was happy to let me take charge of the household." She gave Josie and me a firm look. "I won't be handing over control of the family home to Wendy anytime soon. She and I are very different women." She walked down a hall. Josie and I hurried after her.

We entered the oversized kitchen, then into a butler's pantry. One side was lined with shelves that held trays, serving bowls, and platters of silver and porcelain. "Here we are. I thought the silver platters would be best for the engagement party. Durable."

I said, "It's very kind of you to allow me to use them for the desserts."

She looked at us, her brows knitting together. "Why wouldn't we? There's no use in them sitting here gathering dust and tarnish. The way I look at it, they're too beautiful not to use." Pressing a finger across her lips, she lowered her voice to a hush. "But I didn't want the china leaving the house. Eunice is a lovely lady, but this set is over two hundred years old—hand-painted porcelain, and it's utterly irreplaceable."

I nodded. "I completely understand and wouldn't want it out of my home either."

Josie asked, "Do you use it at all?"

She beamed, pride oozing from every fiber. "Every holiday, birthday, christening, and other special family dinners. Our staff takes extra care with the family china. It's an heirloom that's passed down to the next generation, and I won't take the chance of anything happening to it on my watch."

"Mom?" a deep male voice called out.

"In here." She smiled. "That would be my son, Adam, Andrew's twin."

He jogged into the room and slowed to a confident walk when he saw us. Tall and athletic, he moved with grace and confidence; his jeans and polo shirt were pressed yet casual. Tousled, dirty blond hair was trimmed short on the sides and slightly longer on top. His blue-green eyes twinkled as he bussed his mother's cheek, the kind of son who remembered his manners no matter who was in the room.

"Sorry, Mom. I didn't know you had company." He gave Josie and me a warm smile. "Wait, I know you. Temperance, the baker and former FBI agent. Mom sent me a link to your website once Wendy had decided on the dessert menu." He leaned in and gave Josie a one-armed hug. "Josie, it's been awhile."

"Adam, it's probably ten years, maybe more."

"Yeah, I've been living in Austin. But with Andrew getting married, I decided to come home for a few months so I'll be here through the wedding." He smiled. "I'm a freelance photographer, so I work where I want. Currently, I'm working on gathering enough prints to fill a gallery for a new show."

Josie said, "Congratulations. I had no idea you were still into photography."

"It's how I make a living." He chuckled. "Andrew got the business genes from Dad, and I got Mom's creativity. We're the perfect complement to each other." He shrugged. "Twins in looks only. Most people think we're identical, but we're fraternal."

"Your mom said you were Andrew's twin."

"The better-looking one." He gave us a saucy wink, "And still single."

I felt a rush of heat flush my cheeks. Was he flirting with me? "Noted."

Cissy said, "Adam, you're just in time to help. Temperance and Josie are here to pick up the silver trays for the party."

His smile dimmed as he glanced at his mother, then it changed back to a smile. *What was that all about?*

"Temperance, how many do you need?"

"Four or six if that's not too much trouble."

He grabbed four round and two rectangular trays. "Will these be enough?"

Cissy said, "Ladies, will six do?"

Josie nodded. "Temperance can fill three and have another three on standby in the kitchen."

"That's right." I said, "Cissy, they'll be perfect for the event."

She arched a brow. "You'll be responsible for bringing them back on Monday?"

"The party's tomorrow, if you'd prefer, I can bring them over on Sunday."

She shook her head. "That's not necessary. I'm not sure who's staying with us over the weekend. Since they'll leave right after breakfast on Monday, that will be fine if you drop by then."

Adam asked, "Who's coming?"

"Your cousin Ken is in town, and I'm guessing he's broke again since he asked if he could stay. Money slips through his fingers like vapor; he can't hold onto it. Anyway, I think he's bringing his latest girlfriend, but I'm not sure."

"Perfect, he's in love again. Just what we need. Are Aunt Kathy and Uncle Paul here yet?"

She placed a hand on his arm. "We can talk about the onslaught of relatives later and not bore Temperance and Josie. Now, Adam, take the trays. The girls and I will be right behind you."

He tucked the top six platters under his arm. "Is your vehicle unlocked?"

"Yes, just put them in the back. Thanks for your help, Adam."

Cissy smiled. "Josie, I wanted to thank you for redesigning the invitations. Having the family crest on them is important to my husband." Her tone had an edginess that hadn't been there before.

"It's no trouble. I'll need to remove the floral design I originally had at the top and replace it with the crest. I might need to redraw it if the resolution on the file I have is too low to print properly."

"Do whatever needs to be done and send the invoice to me."

"Don't worry, Cissy. I'll make sure it's perfect. Would you like me to email you a copy before it goes to the printer? I'm going to email a copy to Wendy."

"That won't be necessary. She can approve it. Will the printer rush them? We need to drop them at the calligrapher's early next week."

Josie said, "I was guaranteed that the invitations, response cards, and envelopes would be ready for pick up by midday on Wednesday."

She pressed a hand over her heart. "Thank you. It makes me feel better to know you have it under control."

"Not to worry. I'll have it completed and sent to Wendy by dinner."

"Temperance, it was a pleasure to meet you." She shook my hand.

"Cissy, your home is lovely, and thank you for sharing the platters. It will give the display just the right umph."

She shook Josie's next. "Josie, thank you for your hard work with the invitations."

Adam jogged up the steps and smiled. "I noticed you have a blanket in the back, so I wrapped the trays in it so they won't clang around."

Smiling, I said, "I appreciate that."

Cissy and Adam waved from the steps as we got in, and I drove down the long, winding driveway. With a glance in my rearview, they were still there. I said, "Cissy doesn't seem to be a fan of Wendy."

"I got that same vibe. Possibly Adam, too. Did you see that look he gave his mother when she mentioned the party? I'll go out on a limb and say that Wendy was told to have the crest on the invites and decided she wanted the floral pattern instead. Guess we know the hierarchy of the Posey family."

"Why wouldn't they like her?" I asked.

"You've talked with her a few times; she's a bit… much."

"Yeah, but isn't the most important thing that Andrew loves her and wants to marry her?"

"You'd think." Josie looked out the window as the GPS announced a left turn.

"Adam was charming as ever," she said.

"He's very good-looking. Did you two ever date?"

"No. I wasn't his type. Tall, blonde, smart, and pretty— you know, the kind of woman every guy wanted to date? Kind of like you."

I didn't respond to the hint that I might be Adam's type. "Is Andrew like that? Maybe Wendy is insecure, and marrying into that family must be a bit overwhelming."

"Possible. But either way, she should go with the flow for the next eight weeks until she walks down the aisle. Show Cissy she's an asset to Andrew, not an albatross."

I smiled and put my blinker on when I saw the sign for Oak Hollow Hideaway Inn. My tires crunched over the gravel driveway. "I'm surprised the engagement party is here and not in the gardens at Andrew's home. Not that the inn isn't charming, but... I'll bet the gardens are lovely at the Posey house."

"I get what you're saying. Perhaps this was very important to Wendy; I think she booked all the rooms for both the party and the wedding. It's a nice boon to Eunice's business. She's had a rough time after her husband died. I've helped her with some advertising and her website."

"That was nice of you."

She said, "Eunice is a nice lady. When you meet her, you'll see why."

I popped the hatch and we got out. The inn was eerily quiet. With a quick glance around, I asked Josie, "Is it normally like this on a Friday?"

She looked at her watch. "Check-in is after four, so this must be the lull."

I picked up the platters, and she closed the hatch. "Do you have time to bake brownies with me when we get back?"

She shook her head, "I don't think so. If I need to redraw the crest and still get the files to the printer, I'll be tight on time. And if Wendy won't approve them fast, I'll need to ask the printer for an extension while still hitting the deadline for Cissy."

"Then Hank and I'll walk over after dinner with the treats I promised you."

She grinned. "That will make the afternoon fly, anticipation of dessert."

THERE WAS a note on the front desk saying Eunice was in the kitchen. The first floor of the charming inn was filled with overstuffed chairs and sofas, offering a view of the lush flowerpots and access through glass doors to a wide porch. We walked through the old-fashioned swinging door. The older woman, who was around fifty, was nearly six feet tall, with her gray-streaked blonde hair twisted into a messy bun. She wore a white T-shirt covered with flour and cocoa, stamped with the inn's logo peeking out from a red apron tied loosely around her waist. A smudge of cocoa was on her cheek as she scooped dough into muffin pans.

"Hi, I'm Temperance Matthews, and you know Josie Shaw."

"I know Josie." She smiled. "Hello, girls."

"Mrs. Posey asked if we could drop these trays off for my dessert display for tomorrow."

She beamed, "That was thoughtful of Cissy." She nodded to a table along the back wall. "Temperance, that will be your station for set up and storage."

I placed the trays on the long counter. "Thanks. Will there be room in the walk-in for the dessert? The cheesecakes will need to be kept cool."

"Yes. I've labeled shelf space for you. Take a peek and make sure its adequate. The catering company is bringing a truck that has its own refrigeration, so it's just food for the inn and you."

I pulled open the large steel door and flicked on the light. On the left were two shelves with paper labels; 2.O. I smiled, despite everything, it seemed my little bakery was fast becoming known as 2.O and not the Early Rise or even Little Bakery. The rest of the walk-in seemed empty for a busy inn. Maybe the delivery was coming later today or very early tomorrow.

"That's more than enough space, Eunice. Thank you."

She smiled and wiped her arm over her forehead. "I'd visit, but I'm running behind. We're going to be full up by six and I still need to bake the welcome cookies as well as get the breads and muffins ready for tomorrow."

"Can I help?" I asked.

Eunice hesitated and frowned. "No, thank you. I'll be fine."

With an easy grin, I said, "I happen to be pretty good at mixing batter."

She shook her head. "What I get done, I get done. I'm the only one putting pressure on myself. The guests won't know if there aren't warm cookies at the desk promptly at four."

My gaze swept the tidy space. "Do you have kitchen help?"

Again, she shook her head. "Typically, I have someone baking, but she quit two days ago and I haven't had a chance to look for her replacement."

Josie gave me a nudge and slightly bobbed her head to Eunice.

I took a step forward. "How about I whip up a few items and drop them back later, for breakfast tomorrow? My bake list is almost complete."

Her eyes widened. "I can't ask you to do that."

I gave her a reassuring smile. "You didn't, I volunteered. Just tell me what you need for your guests and I'll make it happen."

Her gaze darted around the kitchen, and she pressed her lips together before saying, "I'd need two banana breads, a large coffeecake, and four quiches."

"Any special kind?" Her request was basic. Doing a quick inventory in my head, I had all the necessary ingredients.

Her shoulders relaxed. "Anything. Are you sure, Temperance?"

Nodding, I said, "Positive. I can be back between six-thirty and seven tonight."

She rushed around the counter and threw her arms around me. "You'd be a lifesaver. Come to the back door. It will be easier to unload your car."

When she released me from her bear hug, I said, "If you think of anything else, give me a call." I withdrew my business card and handed it to her.

"You've saved my life today." She cupped my cheek.

"Sometimes the best answer just walks through the door when you least expect it."

Josie said, "You won't be sorry, Eunice. Temperance's quiche is the best I've ever eaten."

A sparkle lit the older woman's blue eyes. "I'm sure it is. Now, you let this woman finish her cookies, and I'll see you later."

We said our goodbyes and walked back through the main floor and onto the porch. The gardens swept off to the right, down a gentle incline to a gazebo. There were tables and chairs set up under a large white tent. "It's going to be a beautiful setting for the party. I wonder what colors Wendy and Andrew have chosen as their theme."

"I'm not sure. The invitations are white with black lettering, and the crest will be gold. Hey, if you need a helper tomorrow, I'm free."

I snickered, "That's because you want to see how Wendy's organized the party."

"Guilty. Why should you have all the fun? Who knows, maybe I'll get to see Adam again."

I slung my arm over her shoulder. "Is there a lingering crush for that man?"

"No." The way Josie dragged out two little letters made me laugh.

"You know, a thought just popped into my head," Josie said. "You might just get Eunice's weekly baked goods order if this goes well."

"That wasn't why I volunteered to help."

She bumped my shoulder. "I know that, but if it falls into place, it was meant to be."

I laughed. "Come on. We need to get back to town. I have baking and you have design work, and we can't have unhappy clients or even prospective clients."

As I backed the SUV around, a minivan with tinted

windows drove up and parked. People spilled out of the four doors.

A tall, thin man about our age nodded in our direction. He was blond, sporting dark glasses, and bore a faint resemblance to Adam. I waved, and Josie said, "Trouble just blew into town. That's Adam and Andrew's cousin, Ken Grayson."

Looking over my sunglasses, I said, "If that's Andrew's cousin, why is Wendy Carmichael hanging off his arm looking much cozier than a future cousin-in-law should?"

3

————————

$\mathcal{W}$endy caught my eye and casually pulled away from cousin Ken. She was a petite brunette in a floral sundress and wedge heels. "Temperance." She waved. The sun reflected off the ring on her finger, causing it to sparkle as she hurried to the passenger side of the SUV. Through the open window, she asked, "Did you drop off the trays for tomorrow?"

"Yes, we're all set. I have a couple of rounds and rectangles too. The display will be lovely."

She gave a brisk nod. "Everything has to be perfect." Her mouth dipped into a frown. "Josie, how's the revamp of the invite coming along?"

"I'll have a draft over to you shortly. Once you approve it, the printers will have everything ready by mid-week. Cissy mentioned the calligrapher is waiting for them."

Rolling her eyes, she huffed out an exasperated breath, "Everything has to be done by the book. An etiquette book, which is really Cissy's book of rules as a Posey bride. Per my future mother-in-law, the invitations should have already been mailed since we're at the eight-week point." She crossed her arms over her chest and cocked one hip out, "Wouldn't you think if you've been invited to the party tomorrow, you're invited to the wedding?" Throwing her hands in the air, she asked, "Am I wrong?"

I looked at Josie. That was a question neither of us should answer.

"Wendy?" Ken took a step closer and pointed toward the inn.

"Coming." She tipped her head, and her smile returned. "Time to have a little fun."

"Where's Andrew?" I asked.

For a fraction of a second, her smile dimmed, and then she shrugged. "Picking up a few things, he'll be here soon." With a flutter of her fingertips, she skipped back to the group without a backward glance.

"Her mood changes fast."

Josie chuckled. "You got that right."

I waited until the group disappeared around the corner of the porch, except Ken. He stared at us until I backed out and continued to watch until I drove away.

I refocused on the road. "What's up with Ken Grayson? He's a tad odd, don't you think?"

"He's way too cozy with the bride, and what adult skips after the age of twelve?"

"A woman who's very happy. Well, except when I mentioned her fiancé. Did you see her face when I asked about Andrew?"

"I did. And I could tell she wasn't a fan but I had no idea she and Cissy clashed this badly until Wendy was rude about her. Let's just say the wedding vibes aren't great."

I eased onto the main road and headed toward town. "As long as the engagement party goes off without a hitch on my part, I'm happy."

"Drop me at my place so I can work, and don't forget you promised brownies."

Laughing, I said, "How could I forget? Maybe if you get

the crest set and approved, you can ride out to the inn with me later."

"We've got time." She patted her tummy. "If I'm finished and brownies are part of the deal, count me in. I'd do anything for one of your great Aunt Lottie's double chocolate walnut brownies, let alone a plateful."

I pulled up to Josie's house, and she got out, waved, and ran up her front porch steps.

When I parked in my driveway, my contractor and friend, Russ Patterson, was installing my Little Bakery sign on my newly refurbished flower cart. He waved as I got out.

"Russ, this is a surprise." I crossed the grass. "But I can't use the stand until we add the roof to the cart."

He grinned. "I know which is why Erik Wool is stopping by to give me a hand." With a glance at his watch, he said, "I expect him within the next fifteen minutes."

I admired the sign. "The Little Bakery - Early Rise 2.O. It's perfect and I love it." I kissed his cheek. A deep pink flush raced from his neck to hairline. "How can I ever thank you? A check seems inadequate."

"Any chance I could have a cup of coffee while I'm waiting for Erik?"

"Come on in. Do you mind drinking it in the new kitchen? I'm helping out Eunice from the Hideaway Inn with her breakfast for tomorrow. Her kitchen help is nonexistent, and I still have brownies to bake for the Posey-Carmichael engagement party."

Russ walked beside me to the back entrance. "Not at all, and sounds like you're busy. I can sit outside if you'd prefer."

"Nonsense, I'd like the company."

He gave a low whistle as he entered my workspace. "You've done a lot since I saw it last."

"All I've done is put away ingredients and tools of the trade." I looked around, proud of all that I'd accomplished. "I couldn't have done it without your support."

He smiled at the compliment. "It was no big deal."

I placed my hand on his arm, and he looked me in the eye. "It was to me."

He cleared his throat. "I was happy to help."

I flicked the coffee machine on to heat the water as he settled on the stool where Josie had sat earlier. "I'm going to check on Hank."

"Take your time." He smiled. "Do you want coffee? I can make it once the machine's ready."

"Thank you, I would. The mugs and pods are there." I pointed to an open shelf. A muffled series of happy barks came from the house side.

He pointed to the door. "Hank knows you're home."

"He does. I'll be back."

I went into my home kitchen and Hank immediately danced around my legs. His doggy grin caused me to laugh. "Hello, baby. Was I gone a long time?"

He barked again. I carried him outside and placed him in the grass. Nose to greenery, he wandered the fence-line until he took care of business. "Come on, Hank." He dropped to the ground, rolled on his back, and closed his eyes, basking in the afternoon sun.

"I'm leaving the door open." When he didn't move, I slid the magnetic screen door in place, leaving him to sunbathe.

I followed the aroma of freshly brewed coffee. Russ was perched on the stool, holding a mug. He smiled. "Coffee's ready."

I tied my pink apron on and took a sip. Then, I assembled the ingredients for the pie crust.

He looked over the rim of the mug. "It's nice that you're helping Eunice out of a tight spot."

"It's nothing—quiche, a few sweet breads, and a coffee cake."

A twinkle lingered in his eyes. "This is why everyone showed up for you when the fire happened. Since you moved to town and opened the Early Rise, you've given back to the community. And it's why I wanted to help you get back on your feet. Oak Hollow needs more residents and business owners like you."

I lifted a shoulder as I dropped the flour and salt into the food processor, pulsing it for a few seconds, adding the cubed butter and finally the egg and ice water mixture until a lovely ball of dough formed. Working quickly to keep the ingredients cold, I rolled out the crust and fitted the pans before sliding them into the freezer.

"I'm sorry I didn't chat while getting the crusts made. Getting them into the freezer quickly is important."

"Why are you freezing the crusts? Don't you just add eggs and stuff and bake?"

"It produces a more tender crust." I laughed. "There's nothing worse than bad pie crust. When I first made custard pies and quiche, people would often scoop out the filling, scraping the crust in the trash. I knew I had to do better."

"Was that when you opened your bakery?"

I sipped my coffee. "No, when I still worked the government job. The seed of the bakery grew from the baked goods I left in the breakroom at work. After a while, people started asking me to bake birthday cakes, cookie trays, and pies. My boss joked with me that I had opened an exclusive bakery."

He nodded. "That was more than a seed; you were reaping what you had sown. Then what happened? Everyone in town knows Penny Matthews was your aunt but how did you decide to open a bakery here?"

I whisked eggs and cream in a bowl. "I spent summer vacations here as a kid. Penny gets all the credit for teaching me the basics. Coming to Oak Hollow, this became my home." I looked over Russ's head at the door connected to the house. "It was her plan to leave me the house. I only wish I had moved here long ago so that I could have been with her during her final years. A week here and there wasn't enough." I swallowed the lump in my throat. "Penny had a heart of gold."

Quietly, he said, "It runs in the family."

My timer dinged. *Saved by the bell.* "Time to bake the quiche." I withdrew the four pie pans from the freezer, filled each one with the egg mixture, cheese, and a variety of herbs, and then slid them into the oven.

I picked up my coffee mug again. "Anyway, during one of my last visits, we talked about my future. She knew I was miserable, even though I never gave her specifics. That's when she told me I was her sole beneficiary and she wanted me to use this house as a springboard to a happier life." I blinked back the tears on my lashes, hoping Russ didn't notice. "That's how my original bakery came to be, and you know the rest."

"Penny saw a future for you."

Nodding, I said, "I miss her. Can we talk about something else?"

A knock on the door drew my attention. "Come in."

Erik opened the door. He was dressed in dark blue pants and a matching shirt with a logo OHFD on the chest pocket. "Hey. Sorry I'm late." He glanced around the kitchen. "Is Josie here?"

I smothered a grin. He was transparent about how he felt regarding Josie. Too bad she didn't know. "Not right now, she's working."

"Oh, ok. Well, as I was saying, Stu, my replacement, didn't show up on time. Seems he got caught up chatting with an old friend who's back for his brother's engagement party."

"Adam Posey?" I asked.

Erik leaned on the counter. "How'd you know?"

"Josie and I were at the Posey house earlier, and he carried some trays to my car for the party tomorrow."

"He's a good guy. From what Stu said, Adam's staying a couple of months, through the wedding. So, we'll all get together. Russ and you should come, and Josie too." He exhaled as he looked anywhere but at me.

"Yeah, that sounds good. I'll let her know." I cracked a few eggs into a small bowl and whisked them.

Russ said, "We should get out of Temperance's kitchen and finish the roof on the cart."

I gave them a smile and winked. "Stop in before you leave. Who knows? There might be some crumbs that need to be eaten up."

Erik rubbed his hands together. "Now you're saying words I longed to hear." They closed the back door, leaving me to my banana bread batter.

My cell rang. Josie's picture popped up on the screen. I answered her video call. "Hi. Are your ears burning?"

"No. Should they be?"

I grinned. "Erik Wool was just asking where you were."

She practically bounced in her chair. "Really?"

I peeked out the window, but the guys had vanished. "It's like I've been telling you—he's interested, but too shy to make a move."

Her lips curved into a shy smile, and a soft laugh slipped out. "That makes two of us."

"Someone has to make the first move, and I say go for it. Maybe at the party Stu and Erik are going to organize for Adam Posey. "That sounds like fun. In other news, I've finished the invites. Wendy's already approved them and agreed I can have them printed in full color so the crest really pops." Which means," she grinned, "I'm free to be your co-pilot later."

"Perfect. Why don't you come over now? Russ installed the new sign and Erik's helping him with the roof on the flower cart."

She laughed. "Is that your way of giving me a gentle poke?"

I glanced at the screen. "Think of it as a firm nudge. Now

I'm disconnecting, and I expect to see you in my kitchen in ten minutes."

With a playful snort, she said, "Make it fifteen if you expect me to get my flirt on with a handsome fireman. I need to run a brush through my hair."

"Deal. Before you head over, print out the invite. I'd like to see how you tied it all together."

"All right. See you soon." Josie ended the call, and I couldn't help but chuckle. I wasn't sure yet how I'd get Josie and Erik to go on an official date but there was one thing I was certain of—they were perfect for each other. And I wasn't above a little creative matchmaking to make it happen.

A half hour later, the kitchen door swung open. Josie came in laughing with Erik and Russ on her heels.

I had the banana bread in the oven and was testing the quiche. The coffee cake waited on the counter, ready to go in next. "Hey guys, how's the cart look?"

Russ grinned, "Got a minute to come see?"

Josie glanced at me. "I'll stay in here if you need someone to keep an eye on the ovens."

"I have a few minutes." I said, "But first, can I look at the invitation? I've been dying to see how you pulled everything together."

She handed me the paper. "The border's just to show the size for perspective. But you can see it looks sharp."

"I was worried about all the elements, but you've pulled it off—even the book and the rose at the top—the petals are so life-like. The lettering is crisp so I can read every word."

"I'm really pleased with the way it turned out, and I hope Cissy Posey is too. I ended up redrawing the whole thing since the resolution on the file Wendy gave me was too poor to use. It was worth the extra effort, though."

I looked closer. "You're right. The details really stand out."

Passing the paper to Erik, he studied it for a long moment before he handed it to Russ. "This is a little work of art," Erik said. "I've seen the Posey crest on an old banner that used to hang in the game room of the main house, and this looks almost exactly like it."

Josie took the paper from Russ and arched a brow at Erik. "Almost? I was going for exact."

His eyes widened. "Yours is much better. And Temperance is right; the flower's perfect."

Her smile faltered as she glanced my way. "Should I stop the printer? Maybe Wendy didn't look closely when she approved it."

"Josie, it's fine." I hoped my tone was reassuring. "If you're worried, bring this with us tomorrow. After the party, you can show Cissy and get her opinion."

Her shoulders eased. "Good idea. That's what I'll do. Thanks, Temperance, for being a voice of reason."

I smiled, but my gaze drifted to Erik and back to the invitation. "Do me a favor, keep the file Wendy sent you. I have a niggling feeling something is off, and I don't know why—at least not yet."

4

———————

$\mathcal{J}$osie and I arrived at the inn at seven, parking by the kitchen entrance. "Sounds like there's a party going on."

She laughed, hefting the quiche boxes. "It does. I wonder if it's just the people who've come for the engagement party, or if other guests are in the mix."

I opened the door and we entered the kitchen. Eunice bustled around the counter, greeting us with a warm smile. "Temperance, Josie; my goodness." She took the loaves of bread from my hands. "You have no idea what a help this has been. I was able to take a breath this afternoon."

"I'm happy to help. Call me anytime you're in a pickle." I set two boxes of coffee cake on the counter and opened the walk-in refrigerator. "Where should I put these?"

"On the right side. The left is still your spot." She lifted a lid on one of the cakes and inhaled deeply. "This smells heavenly."

"I made an extra just in case."

Josie handed me the boxes of quiche, and I stacked them neatly before closing the door.

"I might sneak a sliver when I'm enjoying my coffee in the morning." Eunice gave me a hug. "Thank you."

The swinging door burst open. "Eunice?" Ken Grayson called, his gaze landed on us. "Oh, there you are."

"How can I help you?" she asked. There was a frostiness in her tone which surprised me.

"Do you have a broom we can borrow?"

"Oh my, did something spill? I'll clean it up."

He grinned. "We're not cleaning, we're doing the limbo and need a pole."

She held up her finger. "I'll be right back." Hurrying from the room, she called over her shoulder, "I've got just the thing."

Ken looked from me to Josie. "You girls should join us. I'm sure Wendy and Andrew would be happy to see you."

Josie's eyes narrowed ever so slightly. She wasn't a Ken Grayson fan. "Thanks, but we need to head back to town. Plans, you know."

He shrugged. "Another time."

Eunice said, "Here you go." She handed Ken a black wooden handle with a smile. "We've had limbo contests here before."

"Great." He nodded his head in our direction, "Ladies," and disappeared through the swinging door.

The three of us stood watching it close. Eunice cleared her throat. "He's having fun."

"Hopefully it winds down before the sun comes up," Josie said.

I chuckled. "If not, the party will be somber and Cissy won't be happy."

"And Wendy will be to blame," Josie added.

Happy to get out of there, I said, "All right, Eunice. I'll see you tomorrow around ten?" I wasn't about to tell her we were asked to arrive at that time.

Her brows drew together. "Why so early? The party doesn't start until two."

"In case you or the caterers need a hand with anything." I said, "Josie's coming too."

"That's nice, but the caterers should have plenty of staff. Come between eleven and half past. That will give you plenty of time to arrange the dessert table and observe the festivities."

"If you change your mind, give me a call. We can be here in fifteen minutes."

"I won't, but thank you." She ushered us out the way we'd come in. "Drive safely."

Josie and I strolled to the SUV when sharp, angry voices reached us. We exchanged a glance and crept forward. Andrew and Wendy were a few yards away, engaged in a heated discussion. His arms sliced through the air, clearly agitated.

"What were you thinking?" he demanded.

"Why are you angry? I did exactly what you said."

He smacked his head. "No, you didn't. I never said for you to become an outrageous flirt with the male members of my family. You're engaged to me, or did you forget?"

"How could I?" she shot back, "With your mother breathing down my neck every two seconds about some ridiculous wedding detail. Cissy's sucking the fun out of everything."

"She's my mother." I heard the warning tone in his voice.

"And she's a pain in my backside. At least Adam and Ken like me."

Andrew groaned, tipping his head toward the sky. "Wendy, all I asked was for you to get along with my family. We need to keep everyone focused on the positives of us getting married while I take care of business that will affect our future."

"Sweetheart, I'm trying, but Ken knows..."

He leveled his gaze on her and took a slow, deliberate step in her direction. "What did you tell him?"

In this dim light, I couldn't see his full expression, but his clenched fists by his sides made my gut tighten. What were they talking about?

She held up her hands and quickly said, "Nothing. I agreed to keep the secret, and I have, but it's getting harder, and after what Cissy had me do today, people might start asking questions."

"What did she ask you to do?'

Wendy put a finger to her lips and lowered her voice. "Someone's coming."

I leaned closer, straining to hear what she said. Instead, I heard, "I found the lovebirds."

A young woman called out as she jogged down the incline. She twirled Andrew around, breaking the tension like a splash of ice water.

"Marie." Wendy greeted her as she grabbed her hand. "What's up?"

"Ken's got the limbo pole and we're ready to dance." She wiggled her hips like she was practicing. "Since Andrew is the reigning champ, I knew you wouldn't want to miss it, and everyone's been looking for you."

"We just needed a few minutes alone." Andrew slipped his arm around Wendy's waist and pulled her close, kissing her cheek.

"Ah, you two." Marie said, "I hope someday I find a guy as terrific as you did, Wendy."

Wendy's smile thinned. "I didn't get the last one. So, there's plenty still out there."

Andrew and Wendy followed Marie up the hill and disappeared around the corner. I pointed to my car, and we hurried back, getting in. With a silent nod, we seemed to agree—not yet. Whatever we had overheard needed to wait a few minutes.

Once we turned onto the main road, I asked, "What did you make of that?"

Josie half turned in her seat. "I'll bet Wendy doesn't want to live at the Posey family home and those two are plotting their way around it—keeping Cissy in the dark until after the honeymoon."

"Would Cissy be upset if the newlyweds found a place of their own?"

"I think it's more than a preference, it's an expectation."

I stared out the windshield. "Isn't that something that went out of fashion decades ago?"

Josie shrugged. "Who knows? But Andrew was pretty worried thinking Adam or Ken might find out."

"Are they the only two male relatives at the party?" I put my blinker on and drove past the police station, wondering briefly if our friend, Officer Casey Butler, was on duty tonight. If she was, chances are she might be called about this party before morning.

"Yes, Cissy and Rob had twin boys, and Ken is Rob's sister's son. Those three are the last of the Poseys."

"Guess they all better have a bunch of kids." I snickered. "Marie might want to try and date either Adam or Ken."

"Out of the three, Adam is the nicest. Ken is lazy and, rumor has it, gambles heavily. That kind of habit can bring more trouble than a declined debit card."

"And Andrew? Decent guy?"

She huffed. "I guess. He's a little arrogant, especially when he thinks he's the smartest guy in the room. Adam, on the other hand, is great. I think that's why he left Oak Hollow. The Poseys can cast a long shadow. "I'm sure nerves about the upcoming wedding are causing some tension, which can happen between couples. New family dynamics can't be easy, either." I slowed, pulled into Josie's driveway, and parked.

"Or living arrangements. But I think, since Cissy married into the family, she understands how difficult it must be to move into an established household."

I nodded. "I'm sure you're right. Pre-wedding jitters. Hopefully, tomorrow, Andrew and Wendy can relax and enjoy the day with their friends and family."

Josie opened the door. "What time are we leaving?"

"I'll pick you up at ten. Call me a worrywart, but this is my first event since the fire, and I want to make sure everything is perfect."

"How about I come over, help you load up, and we can leave your place when we're done."

I placed my hand over my heart. "Josie, you're the best."

She picked up the plate of brownies from the console between us. "I've got to earn my brownie privileges somehow." Before she closed the door, she said, "See you in the morning."

I waited until she was inside and had clicked on a living room light before I backed into the street and headed home. I couldn't get the argument between Andrew and Wendy out of my mind. *Am I being too analytical? A secret doesn't have to be bad. Right?*

THE NEXT MORNING, I walked Hank and snuggled him in for the day with his favorite toys, fresh water, and a new Kong stuffed with peanut butter. I noticed Josie heading up the driveway past the kitchen window. I unlocked the door and held it for her.

"Good morning," she grinned. "You look cute in your logo apron, and that logo is a masterpiece. Who designed it?"

I poked her arm. "I've got an apron in the bag for you, too. Actually, I packed extra in the tote bag in case we get messy."

She scanned the counters. "What needs to go into the back of your car first?

"Everything that's packed in boxes on the counters and refrigerator has to go. The order doesn't matter, but I'm going to start it up and run the AC for a bit first." I pointed to the pot. "We've got time for a cup of coffee if you'd like."

She shook her head. "I'm all set. Do you want one?"

I reached for a mug. "Might as well. Something tells me today isn't going to go as planned."

"I hope you're wrong. It's a beautiful day for the party."

I heard the doorbell. "I'll be right back." I handed her the mug.

She said, "I'll make the coffee."

I hurried through the house while Hank snored in his bed. So much for a watchdog. I saw Casey standing on the porch thorough the window still dressed in her police uniform.

"Morning, Casey, this is a surprise."

"Long night. Any chance I can beg a mug of coffee off you? I need to be around normal people before I go home and crash."

I opened the door wider. "Come on in. Josie's in 2.O making coffee. We're going out to the inn soon to set up for the party."

She grinned. "I like how you refer to the new space. It's fun.

"Let's go back. I'm sure I've got something to nibble on."

With a sharp exhale, she said, "Don't go to any trouble. The coffee will be enough."

I laughed. "Thanks for considering us normal. Why are you late getting off shift?"

Josie looked over, added another mug under the machine, and dropped in a new pod. "Good morning, Casey."

She smiled. "Hi Josie."

"The party you're serving dessert to got a little out of hand last night. We had several noise complaints from the neighbors. The first call came around midnight, so I went out and asked them nicely to keep it down. The second call came at two. One more time, I went out there and reminded them again; people were trying to sleep."

My brow arched. "Let me guess, you had to go out a third time?" I pointed to Josie. "We saw them in action and wondered how long the party would last."

"I broke it up around three. I felt bad for Eunice. Each time I went out, she said she had tried, but they wouldn't listen. To be honest, I think she's happy to have the business and will let the guests do whatever they want just to keep them happy—and maybe get some repeat business down the road."

Josie handed Casey the coffee. "Did you have to arrest anyone?"

"No. Andrew Posey shut it down and sent everyone to their rooms, and he and Wendy left."

I filled a plate with muffins, scones, and brownies and set it on the counter. "When the hosts leave the party, it's time to call it a night."

Josie's eyes lit up at the brownies, and Casey selected a scone.

I said, "Let me know what you think of the scones. They might be on the new menu."

She broke off a corner and popped it in her mouth. "So good with just a hint of lemon. They're a keeper."

"Thanks, I'm glad you like them." I sipped my coffee. "Did you notice a strain or edginess between Andrew and Wendy when you were at the inn?"

She narrowed her eyes and slowly shook her head. "I didn't talk to her any of the times I was out there. Just Andrew and his brother Adam. You know, I didn't realize how much they looked alike until tonight. Probably because I'd only met Adam once during the holidays last year. The Poseys hold a party for the town's emergency personnel."

"That's nice that they do that," I said.

"It is. Adam told me the first time I was at the inn, they'd shut the party down if it got too wild. But I knew by the smirk on Ken Grayson's face that wasn't going to happen." She yawned, popped the rest of her scone in her mouth and drained her coffee. "I'm going to head out. Thanks."

I couldn't help but notice the faint shadows under Casey's eyes. Despite her easy smile, she looked like she knew the chaos wasn't truly over…just on pause.

5

———

*W*endy rushed toward my SUV the moment we parked near the kitchen door, her eyes wide.

"Temperance, thank heavens you're here." She looked over her shoulder. "It's a madhouse. The caterers have just arrived, and guests will be here in three hours. Nothing is ready."

Josie glanced at me as she picked up one of the boxes of petit fours. "Have the flowers arrived?"

She nodded. "Yes, but they're not right. I ordered a summer mix for the large planters at each entrance, which should be filled with roses and a mixed bouquet. There are lilies in the mix. Funeral flowers. Can you imagine?"

"Wendy, I'm not sure what you want me to do. I've brought the desserts and will make sure that the table has an enticing display. Don't you have a party planner?"

She flung her hands in the air. "The one Cissy hired. All he's done is walk around with a clipboard, checking things off, and moving potted flowers. But the linens aren't in place yet. This is going to be a disaster, and Cissy's going to blame me."

I raised a brow, and Josie smothered her smile.

"No. If things are in disarray, the planner will be in the hot seat." I hefted a stack of boxes. "We need to get these inside before the frosting melts off."

She stepped back, but didn't offer to help, which was fine; at least she wasn't blocking the walkway anymore.

The kitchen door was held open with a green brick with looping florals. When we walked in, I noticed the kitchen was buzzing with activity. A low hum of chatter, trays and dishes clinking, and the rich scent of fresh-brewed coffee. To my untrained eye, things seemed to be running smoothly. Not what I had expected after Wendy's description. A tall man, wearing a white polo shirt and black slacks, carrying a clipboard, cut across the room to intercept us.

"Hello, I'm Max Griffin, from Tailored Events."

"Temperance Matthews, Early Rise Bakery, and this is Josie Shaw, graphic designer and dessert delivery gal."

His gaze flicked to his notes. "Excellent." He gestured his pen toward the space Eunice had reserved for me. "You can work there, and I believe the shelves on the left in the walk-in are designated for you."

"Thank you." I wasn't going to burst his self-important bubble, that I was aware of the arrangements. After all, he was doing his job and wouldn't have been briefed that I had been here yesterday to drop dessert trays off.

Josie and I stored the first boxes in the refrigerator and went back outside in the late morning sun. The weather was glorious for the party.

Josie picked up another stack of boxes. "I'm not sure what Wendy was talking about. Max Griffin seems to have everything under control and no one is standing around twiddling their thumbs."

"Nerves," I said, "She's high strung. Remember last night during the argument with Andrew she said that Cissy was going to blame her for something and that was the same phrase she just used. Now, she's tiptoeing on eggshells, trying to impress her future mother-in-law." I scanned the space in the lower garden where a white tent rippled in the breeze. "Isn't that Adam Posey down there taking pictures?"

"It is." Josie stepped away from the vehicle, lifted her arm, and waved. He returned the gesture. "I wasn't aware he was the photographer for the event."

"Maybe he's taking pictures for artistic purposes. The gardens are lovely." I lifted a stack of boxes and walked down the path to the kitchen.

"I'm going to chat for a minute. Be right back."

I smiled. "Take your time."

Once in the kitchen, the staff seemed to have multiplied in the few minutes I'd been outside. Max kept the flow moving. "Two people on linens under the tent and two on the bar set up." Four people volunteered and walked outside.

He nodded in my direction. "Temperance, do you need help unloading your car?"

"No, thank you. I have one more trip, but where should I set the dessert table?"

"Lucia will take you down and show you." He twirled around. "Where's Lucia?"

"Max, I'll be back in a few." I eased out the door concerned I might get caught in a meltdown from someone in that room.

Adam and Josie had met half way and he was smiling and laughing. Josie waved me to join them. Torn between being friendly or getting the rest of the desserts in the refrigerator, I figured a couple minutes being social wouldn't hurt. Jogging down the slope, I reached them in moments.

I grinned. "Hi Adam. I wasn't expecting to see you so early."

"Temperance, hello. As I was telling Josie, I've wanted to do a photo exhibition on flowers for a while, and there's just something about flowers in New England. With the right angles and lighting, they almost breathe from the frame."

"The gardens are stunning. I can see why Wendy and Andrew wanted to have their engagement party here."

His eyes widened briefly. "Wendy didn't. Mom did. She's always liked Eunice and her late husband, Fred, and thought filling the inn with guests and this additional event would be good for many reasons."

"It's nice she wanted to support Eunice." The second part of the statement tickled my curiosity, but I wasn't about to ask what the reasons were. "Are you taking pictures of the party too?"

He raised his hands and shook his head. "Are you kidding? I'd have to deal with my brother's future wife. No way. I'm not saying I won't get a few candid shots of the family, but I wasn't about to hear she wasn't happy with the photos for the rest of my life. I even suggested several excellent photographers. Still, she went off and hired someone I had never heard of."

I hid a smile behind my hand.

Adam said, "No reason to be discreet when it comes to talking about Wendy. We all know what she's about. Too bad my brother is blind to her gold-digging ways. She's all about wanting to get ahead."

Unsure how I should respond, Josie spoke up. "If you need a sugar fix, make sure to hit up the dessert table. Temperance's baked goods are to die for. Especially the brownies, and they're frosted, too."

He smiled. "Good to know. Chocolate and I are best friends, and brownies are my favorite. I'll be sure to have several." Something drew his attention over our heads. "I'll need to go. My cousin seems to be upset about heaven only knows what."

He jogged up the hill and we followed at a more leisurely pace. I said, "Once again, Wendy's not coming off in the best of light with the Posey family."

"Adam thinks she's a gold digger. That puts an interesting

twist on things." Josie glanced around. "I wonder, where is she?"

"Probably getting ready for the party." I nodded toward my car. "One more trip and we're done unloading."

"I can't wait to get a closer look at the trays Cissy wanted you to use. They must be special."

"I'm going to cover the actual trays with linen napkins. Just in case someone uses a fork or knife, I don't want anything to mar the finish."

We reached the SUV and took the last six boxes of tiny desserts. I heard a scream and we hurried inside.

Max was helping Wendy to her feet. "Who was the idiot who used a brick to hold the door open?" She brushed off her knees and glared at Max. "It's a good thing I didn't skin my knees or worse. It wouldn't look good for the bride to be banged up and bruised in a beautiful sundress."

Max said, "I'm sorry, Wendy. If I had known you'd come into the kitchen while we were preparing, I would have informed you. I thought you were enjoying time with your bridal party."

His face remained blank and his voice was devoid of emotion. Neither being over solicitous or dismissive—just perfectly polite. The kind of neutral response that made it hard to guess what he was really thinking. Still, I was willing to bet he didn't appreciate her tone of voice even if he'd never admit it.

I set the boxes aside and took Wendy's arm. "Let me help you to the sitting room. I'll take a look at your knees and sit with you while you relax."

Josie said, "I'll bring in a cup of tea."

She glanced at Josie. "Better lace it with a shot of brandy."

I slipped my arm under Wendy's and escorted her from the kitchen. I felt Max's gaze on my back. Josie called after us, "I'll be just a minute."

Wendy walked with sure and steady steps. There was

nothing wrong with her knees. She was trying to rile up the event planner…but for what end goal, I couldn't tell.

She sat down on the plush tan velvet sofa and stretched her legs out on the table in front of it. "How do they look?"

"Your knees?" I examined them. "Not a scratch; they're not even pink."

She dropped her feet to the floor, the heels on her sandals smacking against the wood. "He's lucky."

"What were you doing in the kitchen?" I kept my tone gentle and watched her closely.

"Checking on the progress for the party. I'm concerned we're going to have a problem today. If I stay on top of every detail, it should go without a hitch."

"Otherwise, Cissy might hold you responsible for any glitches?"

Her eyes narrowed. "What makes you say that?"

"You've said it a couple of times." It got her attention, and I was pleased. "Andrew seems like a great guy but it must be challenging marrying into the Posey family."

She rolled her eyes. "You have no idea the stress I'm under."

Josie came in carrying a mug. "Here you go," she said setting it on the table.

Wendy stood. "Thanks for coming to my rescue in there. I'm going to take a hot shower and get ready." She left without taking the tea.

Josie crossed her arms and watched Wendy dash up the stairs. "So much for a kind gesture and being injured."

I waited until she was out of sight before I said, "It was a performance, but I can't quite figure out the reason." An uneasy feeling lingered as I forced a smile. "Come on, let's get the desserts arranged and under the tent before something else happens."

• • •

THE AFTERNOON SLID by like ice cream on a hot day: sweet and gone too soon. Cissy crossed the lawn toward Josie, and I was consolidating the trays with the last of the desserts, except for a few in the kitchen. The tiny desserts had been a huge hit.

"Hi ladies."

I looked up from the dessert tray. "Hello, Cissy."

Josie said, "Hi Cissy, it's been a wonderful day for your family."

Her gaze followed as Andrew and Wendy strolled hand in hand. "It's been memorable."

She looked at me. "Temperance, Adam asked if by chance there were any brownies left. If there are, would you box them up for him? He said they're the best he's ever eaten and although I'm allergic to chocolate and couldn't try one, I'll take his word for it."

"I'd be happy to. I can include a few petit fours if you'd like. Not a sprinkle of chocolate in those."

Her eyes sparkled with mischief. "I wouldn't say no. But can you wrap them separately? Just to be safe."

"Of course. I'll leave two containers in the kitchen and you can pick them up before you leave."

"Thank you—and Josie, I appreciate that you redid the invitations for a second time. Wendy said they were perfect."

"It wasn't any trouble and I printed out a copy to show you." Josie withdrew the paper from her apron pocket and handed it to Cissy. "What do you think?"

Her face reddened, and the paper shook in her hand. "Wendy gave you the artwork?"

"Yes, ma'am. Is there something wrong?"

"Yes, but not your fault. It's all her." Whirling around, she threw the invitation to the ground and stormed off in the direction Andrew and Wendy had walked.

"That can't be good." I finished combining six trays into two. "Josie, I'm going to clean these up and make up two small boxes for Adam and Cissy from the last of the stash in the kitchen. Can you keep an eye on things here?"

I darted my eyes in the direction that Cissy had gone, and Josie nodded. "Sure thing."

She knew exactly what I was trying to say without words.

"I'll be right back."

Most of the guests had left, but a few lingered on the porch, enjoying a cocktail. They must be staying at the inn.

Max came around the far corner of the building, clutching his clipboard, running a hand over the front of his crisp white shirt and pale blue linen blazer. I had been so busy that I never noticed he had changed clothes.

He smiled. "May I have a few business cards? I have several clients I'd like to recommend your tiny dessert trays to for upcoming events."

"Absolutely. I have some in the kitchen, if you'd like to follow me."

He held open the lobby door, and we entered. The cool interior was a welcome respite from the bright sun.

"How do you think the party went?" I asked as we entered the kitchen.

"Flawless. The caterers did an excellent job, the food got rave reviews, and I even overheard Andrew talking with Adam a few moments ago, and they agreed it was a smashing success."

"I spoke with Cissy, and she's very pleased. Are you planning the wedding as well?"

He nodded as I handed him my business cards, and he slipped them into a folder on his clipboard. "I am. That will be held at the Posey family home. Not that the bride wanted to have the wedding and reception there, but it was the ideal location."

"I agree." I folded two fresh bakery boxes, filling one with a small assortment of non-chocolate treats and the other with just brownies. Max gave me a quizzical glance.

"They're for Cissy and Adam."

"Very good. I'm needed outside." He exited through the back entrance, and I took the platters to the sink to wash and dry them before sliding them into the protective cloths.

As I ran the water over the round tray, engraved with the family crest, something caught my eye. Frowning, I held it up and looked closer. Patting my pocket, wishing I had kept a copy of the invitation. This looked different. But how?

I pulled out my cell phone and snapped several pictures before drying it. I had just finished cleaning up the others when a heart-wrenching scream shattered the afternoon.

"ADAM!" A woman's voice sliced the air like an unstoppable avalanche.

I dropped the towel and bolted out the back door, scanning left and then right. My breath caught—Cissy was crouched over the still form of her son.

"Adam, open your eyes!" She clutched his hand, panic lacing her trembling words. "Help! Someone call for help." Her eyes locked on mine.

I was already calling 9-1-1 as I hurried to her and knelt on the ground.

Adam's face was chalk white, the collar on his pale green shirt was darkened with blood, and a half-eaten brownie was in his hand. The once green-painted brick was beside him, and a smear of red marred the surface. I pressed my fingers to his neck. No pulse.

A voice in my ear said, "What's your emergency?"

"This is Temperance Matthews. I'm at the Oak Hollow Hideaway Inn, and I need the police and an ambulance. Adam Posey has been attacked." I swallowed hard. "I think he's dead."

6

———

*J*osie and I stood a few steps back from the body. From there, I snapped photos of the scene and the people surrounding the scene. Nothing like death to bring out the ghoul in everyone. However, one of them was the killer. Adam hadn't slugged himself with a brick.

Max Griffin flapped his hands, shooing his catering staff closer to the kitchen door, and Ken Grayson nursed a cocktail glass in his hand; an air of disinterest clung to him.

Eunice wrung a dish towel so tightly I thought it would rip in half, as she intermittently dabbed her tear-filled eyes.

Rob Posey held Cissy against his chest, her face buried in his shirt, the raw grief in her sobs filling the silence.

Off to the side, Andrew and Wendy stood apart from everyone else. She hugged herself as if she'd shatter, and her green sundress was mussed. His face was drawn, hands shoved deep into his pockets. They weren't the picture of a couple trying to console each other but stood as lone sentries watching.

Several police officers had strung yellow crime scene tape around a large perimeter, the yellow vinyl fluttering in the gentle breeze like the petals of a nearby flower shaken loose from its pot. The bright slash of color against the horrible scene only magnified the grim reality—Adam Posey was dead. Casey crossed the grass and leaned close to speak with Cissy and Rob in a low tone. She gestured to the inn. After a long hesitation, the couple gave a weary nod and walked beside her. Shoulders bowed inward, steps heavy as if each step pressed their grief deeper into their soul.

I watched Casey, waiting to catch her eye. She gave a slight dip with her chin, my signal to look around and report back any findings. I touched Josie's hand. She followed me away from the crowd so that we could speak freely.

For my ears alone, Josie said, "This is awful. Why would someone want to hurt Adam?"

"The question of the hour." I scanned the tent area. Ken Grayson had relocated to the bar. "Let's start with him."

Max intercepted us before we reached the tent, his face blotchy and his pale blue blazer rumpled. He wasn't the picture of composure. "Temperance, this is awful. Nothing like this has ever happened at an event I planned." His voice cracked as it dropped to a whisper. "Do you think I can let the staff leave? I don't want to end up paying them overtime." He sucked in a ragged breath, eyes darting to the group hovering near the kitchen door.

I stared at him. A man lost his life, and Max was worried about money?

Josie said, "Max, you need to speak with Sergeant Franklin. He's in charge of the scene."

He turned around and looked at the knot of police officers and onlookers. He straightened his shoulders and took a hesitant step in that direction. "Temperance, I've heard about the two previous cases in town where you assisted the police in solving them. Since you've got a good rapport with them, would you mind asking them? It might go better coming from you."

"No, Max, I'm not going to run interference for you with the police." I kept my gaze leveled on him. "In fact, if I were running the investigation, no one would leave until my officers had a chance to question every last person here, and that includes you."

He threw his hands up and slapped them on his thighs. "Oh, come on. You make it sound like I'm responsible for Adam's murder." He rolled his eyes but there was a nervous edge to his tone. "If this drags on, people will talk, and it looks bad for business. The last thing I need is the cops poking around, and that would be even worse."

I cocked a brow and crossed my arms. "Do you have something to tell me about what might have happened during the party?"

He tugged on the collar of his shirt and glanced toward the officers. "Part of my job is keeping my mouth shut. Unless I'm forced to talk under oath, I'm just background noise."

Josie said, "Max, no one is asking you to break a confidence. But a man has been murdered."

He nodded to the tent. "Ask Ken Grayson. I overheard him and Wendy arguing about Andrew and Adam."

"Do you know what it was about?"

"Roses. But that's all I'm saying." He stormed off, and I continued to watch him, but he didn't go talk with the Sarge; instead, he stood with the catering staff.

Josie glanced at me. "What do you make of that?"

"I'm not sure, but guess who just made it to the top of my suspect list?"

We walked to the tent where Ken sat by himself, at a table toying with a glass of amber liquid.

He glanced up. "You can clean up."

"Actually, we shouldn't." I said, "This is part of the crime scene."

"Why aren't you with the family?" Josie asked.

He took a slow sip and watched her over the rim of the

glass. "What's there for me to do? Adam is dead. Cissy and Rob are shattered that one of their precious sons won't reach their full potential, and Andrew just realized everything now rests on his shoulders."

The bitterness in his tone was sharp enough to slice through the tension.

"You didn't like Adam?" I pulled out a chair and sat.

His eyes locked on mine. "That's a stupid question. He was my cousin."

"That doesn't mean you liked him." I kept my voice even, waiting for the tell.

He jumped up from the table, and the chair clattered to the ground. The glass left his hand in a blur, and he flung it against the tent wall, the amber liquid streaking the heavy vinyl before the glass landed in the soft grass. He jabbed a finger at me. "You're outta line."

I righted his chair and tapped the table. "Ken, have a seat."

Josie said, "We're just asking a few simple questions. Ones the police are sure to ask you at some point."

"Why? I didn't kill him." He sank to the chair and dropped his head into his hands. "He should have been taking pictures and planning his show. What did he get himself mixed up in in that someone would want him dead?"

My mind locked on to one detail. *The camera.* Where was it? "When was the last time you saw Adam and did he have his camera?"

He lifted his head and narrowed his eyes. "Why should I tell you?"

Josie said, "Temperance is a former FBI agent and very smart. Something you might say could be an important clue to catch the killer."

Ken sat up straighter and locked his eyes on mine. "If you're so smart, why are you baking cookies for parties instead of solving crimes?" His eyes were clear, so alcohol wasn't the reason for his sharp rebuke.

I measured my words carefully, deliberately adding in a double entendre. "Crime takes a toll on the soul." The man never flinched. Either he was innocent or very shrewd.

"Fine." He crossed to the bar, poured himself another drink, and sat down. "Let's see. It was about an hour ago, and yes, he had his camera, taking random shots of the party. As far as I know, Adam made friends easily. His picture should be in the wiki next to the word saint—and the worst part, he actually lived up to it." He pressed his fingers to his eyes.

The raw emotion Ken displayed made me believe his statement, and when I met Adam, I instantly liked him, too.

"I'm very sorry for your loss, Ken." Josie reached across the table and placed her hand on his arm.

He didn't look up but murmured, "Thanks."

"Ken, did you and Wendy argue earlier?" I asked.

He snorted. "Can you be more specific? That woman's a toxic dump of emotions—we argue every time we're in the same space for more than fifteen minutes."

Josie quirked a brow. "So...you did argue today?"

"Yeah, she was ticked that Adam was taking pictures and Andrew wasn't stopping him."

I asked, "Why would it matter?"

Ken rolled his eyes. "Wendy didn't want him to, and I quote, 'profit off her engagement party.'"

I tipped my head. "Wasn't it *their* engagement party and Adam's family, in fact, her soon-to-be husband's twin?"

"I said who cared if he took pictures of roses." He held up his hands like he was surrendering. "And you're not telling me anything I didn't say to her." He jabbed his finger in the direction of the inn. "If you got questions, go ask her. I've never understood what Andrew saw in her; he's not Wendy's type. But hey, who am I to judge?" He drained the glass.

Josie and I sat at the table for a couple of seconds to see if Ken would expand on Wendy. When he got up to get another drink, I said, "I'm sorry for your loss."

He didn't look at us, held up his hand, and said with a catch in his voice, "Thanks."

We left Ken in the tent lost in the bottom of his glass.

I said, "Wendy didn't make brownie points with any of her future relatives. Yesterday, weren't Ken and Wendy chummy?"

Josie said, "When we were leaving and they arrived?"

I nodded. "Yes."

She said, "If I hadn't known who Ken was, I would have sworn he was Andrew. The way she was clinging to him and that giggle." She rolled her shoulders. "Ick."

My lips thinned. "Exactly. Let's head to the lobby. Oh," I caught her arm. "Do you have a copy of the invitation with you?"

"No." She tipped her head. "Why?"

"When I was cleaning the dessert trays, I noticed the crest looked…different. I couldn't put my finger on what it was. I was hoping to compare them."

"I don't. Did you take pictures?"

"Does sugar go in my sweets?" It felt good to offer a light-hearted quip, even though the circumstances surrounding us were no longer happy.

"We can compare them later. It's probably just a matter of a few tweaks over time. It's not unheard of for family crests to be altered slightly over the centuries."

We climbed the hill. Eunice sat in a lawn chair, and Max was seated next to her.

Neither was speaking. Perhaps it was enough of a comfort just to have someone close by.

"Eunice, are you doing okay?" I knelt next to her chair.

Her voice trembled as she dabbed a tissue to her eyes. "Temperance, this is awful. I know it's a terrible thing to say right now, but what will this untimely death do to my business? Once it's published in the paper—or worse, if it shows up on any travel websites—my bookings could vanish. And just like that," she snapped her fingers, "I could be out of business by the end of the season."

I gave her arm a reassuring pat. "I'm sure it won't come to that. You weren't involved in what happened to Adam."

Max slumped in the chair, his eyes flitting between me and Josie. "Eunice has a point. It could tarnish her inn's reputation or have the opposite effect. Drawing people in to see where the heir to the Posey fortune died. I'd be lying if I said I wasn't worried about my business too."

Eunice bolted out of her chair, her face pinched and blotchy. "Max, that's a horrible thing to say." Her voice cracked, "How could you even think such a vile thing? Profiting off those wonderful people's pain…"

Josie said gently, "Eunice, Max. I know you're both worried, and this has been a shock to all of us. You shouldn't jump to conclusions. Only one person is responsible for what's happened, and unless one of you hit Adam with the brick, you're in the clear, and so are your reputations."

Max gave a quick nod, and he dropped his attention to the grass. He toyed with the button on his blazer. "Yeah…right."

I caught a flash of unease in his eyes as he avoided my gaze. It might be nothing, but I trusted my gut. That kind of reaction could be important later.

Eunice nodded. "Thank you for saying that, Josie. A bit of calm logic was just what Max and I needed. We've been sitting here spinning in worry."

I stood. "We're going to check with Officer Butler and see if there's anything we can do." And I wanted to get closer to the crime scene. I needed more pictures with better angles, and where was Adam's camera? That was a bug I would put in Casey's ear.

Eunice's voice was soft. "I'm sure she'd appreciate your

help. From what I've heard since the bakery fire, you have a way of seeing through the maze of clues and finding the truth."

"Thank you, Eunice—that's a nice compliment, but the police have this under control." There was no way I was letting anyone think I planned to get involved, even though Josie and I were already headed in that direction.

"Temperance? Josie?" Casey stood on the porch and waved us over.

I said, "Eunice, we'll see you and Max later."

Josie and I hurried over the grass as Casey came down the steps. She pointed to an area away from the group.

"How are things going?" I asked.

She shook her head. "Not good. From what everyone has said, Adam was a great guy. I can't find one person to say one negative thing about him."

"So there's no motive?" Josie asked.

Casey said, "Exactly. What have you discovered?"

I slipped my hands into my apron pocket. "We got much of the same from Ken Grayson. Although Wendy was mad that Adam was taking pictures of the flowers. Have you found Adam's camera?"

"Camera? No, why?" she asked.

"Adam's been taking pictures all day, but it's not with his body. That can't be a coincidence, right?"

"I'll alert the officers. They're scouring the grounds for clues. But I need your help."

I pulled my hands free. Being asked to help would make it easier to get around the crime scene.

"Wendy won't answer any questions unless Andrew is out of the room, and he's determined to stay with her. Could you take him aside on the premise of asking him a few casual questions?"

"Consider it done." I scanned the crowd. "Where is he?"

Josie tipped her head toward the rose garden. "Standing beside the roses with Wendy. His back's to us, he's wearing a light green shirt."

My eyes grew wide. "Adam had on a light green shirt, too."

7

———————

$\mathcal{C}$asey looked at me. "Excellent observation. One I'd overlooked." She tipped her head as she looked at Andrew. "Were they identical twins?"

Josie said, "Not from what Adam said, but they look very similar."

"Are you thinking this might have been mistaken identity?" I asked.

She nodded. "We shouldn't rule it out."

"Casey, how do you want to play this, to get Wendy alone?"

Josie said, "The easiest way is to ask Andrew something about Adam, and Wendy can slip away with Casey."

The officer nodded. "I like that approach. But what will you ask him?"

I frowned. *This might be harder than I think.* "I'll think of something."

We walked over to where they stood with the members of the bridal party. I cleared my throat. "Andrew, could we speak with you for a moment? Privately."

"Excuse us." He took Wendy's hand and followed. "What do you need? I can't help you. I'm in the dark as to why

58

anyone would want to hurt Adam. He was a saint, not Satan."

Wendy's gaze darted between us. She licked her lips and tipped her head toward the inn. Casey said, "Temperance and Josie spoke with your cousin, Ken, and they're hoping you could clarify a few things."

"Sure. Anything to help catch the monster who killed my brother."

Wendy pressed a kiss to his cheek. "Andrew, I'll be right back. I'm going to get you a glass of water. You need to stay strong. For Adam." She didn't even blink as the excuse slipped from her lips as if she'd rehearsed it.

"Thank you, Wendy. You're right."

She glanced at me. "Take care of Andrew for me?"

I nodded. "Of course."

After taking a couple of steps, she turned. "Casey, would you go with me? I don't want to answer any questions, and if people see us together, they'll keep their distance."

"I'd be happy to." Casey said, "We'll be back shortly."

Andrew grabbed Casey's arm. "Keep her safe. I couldn't bear it if anything happened to her. Please."

She glanced at his hand on her arm and he let go. She said, "I will protect her."

His plea wrenched my heart. He clearly believed he was shielding the woman he loved, but watching Wendy leave with Casey, I had to wonder, who needed protection: Andrew or Wendy?

"Andrew?"

He tore his gaze from Wendy and said, "What do you need from me?"

"Can we sit over there?" I pointed to a table and four chairs under an ancient maple tree.

He went with us, each step slow. His eyes darted from Wendy to the crime scene tape just beyond the inn.

After he was settled, he asked, "How are my parents?"

"Doing as well as can be expected. Officer Butler reassured them she'll work tirelessly to find out who did this."

He dropped his head in his hands. "Before they attack someone else in my family, you mean."

"Andrew, did your brother say anything to you about trouble? Had he been threatened since returning?"

"Not that I'm aware of. Everyone loved Adam. He was the kind of guy that'd give you his last dollar if he thought someone needed it more than he did. Those kinds of guys don't get whacked over the head."

In this case, the nice guy *did* get attacked. "Has anyone threatened you?"

He blinked and pulled back. "Absolutely not. Now, if you want to look at family members, dig into my cousin, Ken. He's always hanging around shady people. He has an affinity for cards, ponies, and anything else you can bet on. Mom bailed him out for years, being family and all, but she stopped that a couple of years ago and told him to deal with his own mistakes; she was done being his bank account."

"Is there any reason to think Ken is in trouble right now?"

He snorted. "Not at the moment. Wendy took pity on him and bailed him out."

"I didn't know they were close," Josie said.

With a pinched expression, he folded his arms over his chest. "Neither did I." His tone was flat, but the twitch of his jaw spoke volumes.

I asked, "Have you seen Adam's camera lying about?"

He shifted in the chair and looked away.

"Ken mentioned Adam had it the last time he saw him. Now it's missing. I was hoping the police or you might know."

I watched him closely; his body language had shifted the moment I brought it up, like I caught him mid-thought.

"I don't know. It should have been with him." His eyes

flickered toward me, but he wasn't looking at me—over my shoulder was a better description.

"I'm sure it's around here somewhere. Maybe you should ask the event planner. He seems to keep his eye on everything."

That was…curious. "I'll do that. Of course, just to help the investigation."

Josie asked, "How did Wendy and Adam get along? I'll bet she was thrilled to be getting a brother."

He lifted his shoulder in a non-committal shrug. "It was an adjustment being an only child with parents who don't prioritize being a family. Now everything revolves around it."

I filed that away. For a man who seemed aloof, he was very sure about the details that mattered most to him. And that was Wendy.

He stared at the inn. "What's keeping them?"

Josie said, "I'm sure they'll be right back. Perhaps Wendy needed to use the ladies room."

It was a weak suggestion but accurate if one didn't know Casey was taking this opportunity to question Wendy at the bride-to-be's request. "Would you like me to check on them?"

Pushing himself to a standing position, he swayed and clung to the edge of the table. "I'll do it."

Josie and I jumped up. "Andrew, are you alright?"

His face flushed a deep pink as he clung to the edge of the table. "I need a minute."

"Josie, stay with him, and I'll get an EMT."

I rushed to the back of the open ambulance. Dave Buckles was inside. "Got a sec? Andrew Posey was talking with me and Josie, stood up, almost lost his balance, and his face flushed."

"Van, we have a situation." He picked up a blue bag and slung it across his body.

His partner, Van Jones, came around the corner and

grabbed a pack from the ground. They ran alongside me as we threaded our way through a small group of people.

Josie waved us closer. "He's thirsty, can I get him a drink?"

Dave shook his head, "Let us examine him first." He guided Andrew to a sitting position and pressed his fingertips to the underside of his wrist.

"Can you tell me what happened?" Dan asked.

Andrew's voice was hoarse. "My heart's racing and my chest is tight. Am I having a heart attack?" He squeezed his eyes shut. "I feel like I'm going to get sick."

Van leaned in and pressed the stethoscope to his chest, "It's okay if you do."

"What else are you feeling, Andrew?" Dave asked.

"My head hurts, I'm dizzy, my fingers are numb, and I can't stop shaking." Fear seeped into his words. "Where's Wendy? I need her. I'm too young to die." He gave a shaky groan. "Then again, apparently, I'm not. Maybe my parents will be burying two sons."

The tremor in his hands and the color of his face told me this wasn't an act. Andrew was unraveling before us.

"Andrew, have you ever had a panic attack before?" Dave asked.

"Not that I recall." He shook his head. "I'm not having a heart attack?"

"We won't know for sure until we get you to the emergency room," Van said, "but based on this exam, I believe that's what's going on. It's understandable given the amount of stress you're under."

"I'm not leaving the inn. My family needs me. Wendy needs me. Adam—" his voice broke. "Being here, making sure people do their jobs, is the only thing I can do for my brother."

I placed a hand on his shoulder. "He wouldn't want you to not get the medical attention you need."

"I won't die from a panic attack." Andrew shook his head. "I'll be fine, all I need is to see Wendy. Where is she?" Agitation rose in his voice with each word.

Giving his shoulder a squeeze, I said, "Here she comes now, with Officer Butler."

He rose on unsteady legs and stumbled toward Wendy with his arms outstretched as if she could ease the pain with her touch. It might have been a scene right out of a movie, but she didn't fall into his arms. They dropped to his sides, his shoulders slumped under the weight of the moment. His grief was palpable while she remained aloof.

"What took so long?" he asked.

She didn't bat an eyelash. "Everyone wanted to express their condolences about Adam. It took a bit to get to the kitchen." She handed him a glass of water. "Drink this, it might help your stress." With a glance at Van and Dave, she asked, "What are you doing here? Shouldn't you be dealing with," she glanced at Andrew, "the other situation?"

Was it kind of her not to say Adam's name—or was it a lack of real emotion? I wondered what Josie's take would be on this conversation. It was something we'd dissect later.

"I was having a panic attack and they checked me out."

Wendy took his hand. "You haven't had one of those in a long time. Not since before…"

He tugged on her hand and said, "I'm fine."

Van said, "Andrew should go to the emergency room to be looked at, just to be sure it's nothing more serious."

"Andrew, maybe you should. After all, they know more about medical things than we do."

Wrenching his hand from her, he glared at Van and Dave. "I'm not leaving." There was no mistaking the sharpness in his tone. The discussion was over.

Van said, "If you start to feel the symptoms return, you should go to the ER, just to be safe."

He nodded. "Thank you."

The EMTs picked up their gear and crossed the lawn. In Oak Hollow, the ambulance was used to transport both living and deceased individuals.

I didn't think there was much more to learn here. "Josie, we should let Wendy and Andrew talk with their families."

Casey nodded. "If either of you needs anything, call me." She handed each of them her contact card.

Andrew took both cards and stuffed them in his shirt pocket. "Thank you. Will you continue to question our guests?"

"Yes, it's standard in situations like this. It's better than letting people leave and calling them in for a conversation over the next few days. Right now is when the details are the freshest."

"If you need us, we'll be with my parents."

Casey stepped aside, allowing Andrew and Wendy to leave. When they were out of earshot, she said, "For the record, she's one cool lady."

"What did she want to tell you?"

"Ken Grayson's deep into gambling debt. With Andrew and Adam's portion of the Posey empire already accounted for, he wasn't entitled to a single cent, but with one of them dead, that was a different story. He needs access to a lot of money. I'm not sure how, and it's not a question for Mr. and Mrs. Posey today, but soon."

She turned her back on the witnesses. "Did you learn anything?"

"Andrew pointed a weak finger at Max Griffin, and he said Wendy bailed Ken out of some debts, also he didn't know that Ken and Wendy were good friends. That's when he had a panic attack."

She arched a brow. "Do you think it was genuine?"

"Yes." I nodded. "Check with Van and Dave and get their take on the situation. Andrew refused to go to the hospital, stating he needed to stay here and make sure Adam got justice."

Casey's gaze swept the scene. "If you were to say right now who you thought was guilty, and put them in order from one to whatever, give me a rundown."

I thought for a moment. "Ken Grayson, Wendy Carmichael, Max Griffin, Andrew Posey."

Josie's brows lifted. "You think Andrew could have attacked his own brother?"

"Not out of malice," I said, "but they could have argued, and things got more heated. Andrew picked up the brick and hurled it at Adam. One blow to the head caused his death."

"If it was an accident, why wouldn't he say something?"

"Because," Casey folded her arms over her chest. "Even accidents are thoroughly investigated. He could be charged with involuntary manslaughter."

I nodded again, my gaze following Andrew and Wendy as they mingled with the guests as they grew closer to the inn. Smiling and shaking hands like they were working a reception line. Every now and then his smile would falter, but he'd pull his shoulders back and keep on talking. "What exactly does Andrew do for work?"

"He's a vice president of the Posey Development Corporation."

"And Wendy?"

"A commercial real estate agent," Casey replied without hesitation.

Josie smirked as she glanced at Wendy. "That's how they met."

I tilted my head and narrowed my eyes. "And how did you uncover this?"

"Remember when you asked me to refill one of the trays and I went to the kitchen?"

"I do."

"When I was carrying the tray back to the tent, I passed a

couple of the bridesmaids chatting, and they stopped me to get some dessert. They were talking about how *he* was looking to acquire a plot of land, *and* she was the realtor. Love at first handshake."

I murmured, "That's one way to grow the business. I wonder if it's ethical to work together?"

The line between Casey's brows creased. "I'll look into that, see if anyone has filed any conflict-of-interest suits against one or both of them."

My thoughts churned. "Could that be a link to Adam's death?" I snapped my fingers. "Are we certain everyone here is on the guest list?"

She flashed me a small, one-step-ahead-of-you smile that said she already anticipated my question. "I've asked Benson to double-check each person against the guest list. We'll know for sure by the end of the day."

8

———————

"Come with me," I said to Josie. "I want you to see the tray with the different crest before we leave." We skirted the guests who lingered on the lawn. Casey and Sergeant Franklin were releasing people after they had been questioned.

I opened the kitchen door that, only a few hours before, had been held open with the fatal green-painted brick. A shiver raced up my spine. "Josie, was that brick still propping open the door when you came up to refill the tray?"

Her brow furrowed. "I don't think so." She shook her head firmly. "No. Definitely not. I remember pushing it open with my backside when I walked out. If the brick had been there, I wouldn't have had to do that."

I turned sharply. "Where's Max Griffin?"

She pointed over my shoulder. "Under the tent."

"Hurry, before he leaves."

Rushing over the grass, dodging people, I lifted my hand and called out, "Max."

Leaning against the tree, he crossed his ankles as if he didn't have any place better to be. A very different look from earlier, when all he wanted was to leave. His lazy smile didn't

67

reach his cool gray eyes. "Ladies, how can I help you? I assume you're questioning people regarding the recent murder. Don't you know you should leave that to the professionals? You might get tangled up in something that wouldn't be good for your health."

Josie bristled. "Temperance *is* a professional."

His brow shot to his hairline and a smirk graced his lips. "Really? You're a baker."

My fingertips grazed her arm. "We don't need to bore Max with my resume."

He gave me a sidelong glance, the kind that lingered a fraction of a second too long. It wasn't casual curiosity; he was more interested in my past than I wanted or needed him to be.

"Do you remember when Wendy yelled at you about the brick holding the kitchen door open?"

His posture remained relaxed, but when his jaw flexed, I knew I'd hit a nerve. "Wendy didn't need to be rude. That brick had been holding the door open all morning and she was the only person to trip over it."

I remained silent, hoping he would keep talking. Josie did the same. With a huff, he threw up his arms and said, "Fine. I kept the brick in the door out of spite." His eyes narrowed. "However, mid-afternoon, I went to check on the staff, and the appetizers were running low. I saw Josie walk out of the kitchen with a dessert tray and noticed the door shut after her. I looked around for the brick, but it was no longer there. Not that it was a big deal. The party was wrapping up within the hour, and I'd find something to keep the door open before the caterers repacked their vans."

"What time was that?" I asked.

He tapped his finger against his lips. "Around two-fifteen. It's hard to be exact. The party was scheduled to end by four, but people tend to linger." He glanced toward where the crime scene tape fluttered. "Free food and drinks will keep people hanging around."

"And you didn't notice any of the guests near the kitchen?" Josie asked.

With a sharp retort, he asked, "Did you?"

She lifted her chin. "I'm not the one with an axe to grind against the family."

"Neither am I," Max shot back. "There are a lot of bridezillas in the world, and I've worked with them all. Wendy Carmichael isn't the first, and sadly, she won't be the last."

I tipped my head. "Did you know Adam Posey?"

Max shook his head. "No. Not until today when he introduced himself to me and the staff. It seems he wanted to get everyone's permission to take candid photos, and if he wanted to use them in a show, he'd reach out for a signed release."

"Did anyone object?" Josie asked.

I suppressed a smile. Josie was impressive, firing off questions like a pro.

"Once the staff realized who he was, the famous photographer, they were eager to agree." His shoulders slumped, his voice softened. "I was a huge fan of his work. You could see the greatness in his art. It moved everyone who experienced it."

The raw emotion in Max's voice almost made me believe that he wasn't connected to Adam's death. Almost wasn't proof of innocence. "If you think of anything that seemed out of place, will you call me?" I handed him another card even though I was sure I'd given him one earlier in the day.

His eyes met mine. "Shouldn't I call the police?"

"You can, but in cases like this, Josie and I act as consultants."

He quirked a brow. "Because of your background?"

I nodded. *Please don't let him ask any specific questions I don't want to answer.*

"Fine. I'll call as long as it doesn't put me in the hot seat with the cops."

"If you'd feel better, ask Officer Butler or Sergeant Franklin. I'm sure they'll say it's all right."

"You know, there was one person who I think didn't like Adam."

My eyes widened. "Really?"

"Wendy. I overheard her and Andrew talking yesterday when I stopped by to do a walk-through."

I didn't realize he had been here. "Do you remember exactly what was said?"

His mouth curved into a smile. "I have excellent recall. In my business, it helps to remember the tiniest details."

"That's good, but what was said?" Josie prodded.

He continued, "Wendy said it was too bad Adam made it back for the party. She was hoping they'd have more time."

I leaned forward. "More time for what?"

"I'm not sure. When she saw me, she stopped talking. Then Andrew covered by asking if everything was ready for today."

I tamped down my frustration. "Maybe she's been trying to win over Andrew's parents. They don't seem to be Wendy's biggest fans. With Adam home, the focus would shift away from her efforts."

"Possibly. She does love all the attention." He gave a small nod. "Officer Butler's headed this way."

I acknowledge her with a nod. "Officer. We were just talking with Max and said if he recalled anything, he could give me a call."

"Correct," she confirmed. "Temperance and Josie are paid consultants of the Oak Hollow PD and should be viewed as trusted members of the team."

"Good to know." Max looked from me to Josie, "I'm sorry I doubted you."

"No harm done," Josie said.

"Officer Butler," I looked at Casey to keep things very professional. "If you agree, Josie and I are going back to my place."

"Yes, if you could walk the grounds one last time and make sure the items you brought are accounted for?"

I was sure this was code for taking a final look before we left. "Thank you, we'll do that."

Josie and I left Casey with Max.

"What do you make of the Wendy and Adam info?"

"We can only speculate that Wendy didn't like Adam, and there's something she and Andrew didn't want him to know." I glanced over my shoulder. Wendy followed our movements from the porch as we walked the perimeter of the tent. "Don't look now, but someone is keeping an eye on us."

She lowered her voice, "Wendy?"

I walked so I could keep her in my peripheral vision. "Bingo. She might be worried we'll stumble across a piece of evidence that could incriminate her or talk to someone who'd point a guilty finger in her direction."

Josie hesitated. "Andrew was wearing a green shirt nearly the same shade as Adam's. If Wendy was the attacker, either she knew it was Adam and needed to get him out of the way, or she assaulted her future husband. Why would she do that?"

"Money?" I murmured as we walked closer to the remains of the dessert table. I didn't want Wendy to suspect that we were having a conversation. We were the help today, not a dynamic sleuth duo.

"That can't be the reason. As Andrew's wife, she'd inherit money."

"True. As a fiancée, most likely she'd get nothing," I said.

"Unless he's already drawn up a will in her favor," Josie said.

"This is all conjecture until we can talk with Cissy and Rob. They'd know about the Posey estate and if Andrew had money of his own to distribute as he saw fit, and what happens now that Adam's dead, and how will it benefit Ken financially?"

"Do you think there's anything more to be learned from him before we leave?" Josie leaned against the table as Wendy stared.

"Do you think it's a good idea to have a staring contest with your client?" I picked up the last two silver trays, preparing to take them to the kitchen and clean them. Then, I'd put them in my SUV for safety, and it'd give me an excuse to stop and speak with Cissy.

"She doesn't know where I'm looking, but her posture's relaxed. Not at all what I'd expect with a murder committed at her party and a member of the family."

"Shock can do that to a person," I said.

"Or a cold-hearted witch who has no feelings would look exactly like that." Her jaw tightened. "If this is about Adam being *taken care of so* that Andrew and Ken could inherit more money, I hope justice is served swiftly."

She clutched my arm as the ambulance rolled quietly down the driveway, its lights dark and siren silent. There was no sense of urgency. The heaviness of the moment weighed on us both.

I needed to refocus her attention on something that could potentially strengthen the case. "Josie, look at the tray." I handed her the etched silver platter. "Tell me, does it look like the same crest that you put on the invitation?"

She studied it for a moment and said, "No, it doesn't. The top is wrong." She tapped above the shield. "This crest is missing the book and rose impression. Remember the painting in the foyer at the Posey's? The crest on the wall. I wonder if Cissy realizes whoever did the engraving had the wrong file."

"We'll need to find out when the book and rose were added." I filed that away in my mental "something to ask Cissy" folder.

Josie said, "That won't be today. I wonder if I should stop the printer?"

With a side glance, I said, "It won't matter either way. If it's wrong and the invitations are a couple of days later than planned, the family will have more on their mind than a wedding."

"True." She took the tray from me as we walked from the tent back to the kitchen. "When we get back to your place, are we working on the…"

Despite the gravity of the moment, I forced a half-hearted smile. "It's what the situation calls for."

"I'll call in for a pizza and we can pick it up on the way home."

Now I grinned. "You'd better make it a large with a salad. I suspect Casey will be stopping by to see what we've uncovered—and we both know she rarely says no to dinner with us."

Max was still talking with Casey, his arms flailing, his face a deep shade of red.

Josie leaned in. "What do you suppose that's all about?"

Before I could answer, Max's voice cut the din. "I already told you—I didn't lay a finger on Adam. All I did was give him a to-go box of brownies. End of story!"

A ripple of shocked murmurs spread through the last of the partygoers.

Casey spoke with him, gesturing with her hands for him to calm down. I had no doubt her voice was low and soothing as she attempted to de-escalate the situation.

Josie and I exchanged a worried look. "Well," I said under my breath. "That's one way to point the guilty finger at yourself. We'll ask Casey about this later. And we need to get some additional photos of the scene now that they've taken Adam away."

"Let's skirt the outside of the group," Josie said, taking the lead.

I glanced over my shoulder at Casey and Max. His color returned to normal, which was a positive sign. An agitated witness proved ineffective, as details could easily be overlooked during questioning. Casey was good—one of the best—but with someone who was overemotional, even the sharpest investigator could come up short on clues.

Sergeant Franklin met us at the edge of the scene. "Temperance. Josie. Any observations you'd like to share?"

I shook my head. "Not yet, Sarge. There are too many questions and no answers. The only thing we all know is that a man is dead and the killer was here today."

The sergeant turned to the officers. "Give the ladies booties and full access for photos." He turned. "I'm assuming that's what you're after?"

I gave a small nod. "You know me so well. By any chance, did you find the victim's camera? It's a high-end professional version."

A police officer I didn't know by name handed us coverings for our shoes. We donned them, and I withdrew my cell.

Sergeant Franklin said, "Not yet. But we will. It couldn't have gone far. I've had Benson search each car before the guests left, after they were questioned, of course." He turned away.

"Josie, take pictures of everything. If something seems off, take a picture."

"Consider it done." She had her phone out and moved slowly, rapidly tapping the screen.

I stepped back, trying to replay the events in my mind as if I had been the one who had attacked. "Officer." I stopped the young woman who had handed me the booties. "Which way was the victim facing?" Even though I had briefly seen the body, I was intent on scanning the crowd, not the details about Adam.

She frowned as if uncertain. "Toward the tent. The box of brownies tumbled open in that direction, too. Is it important?"

I nodded and strode to the shed. "Very. Theoretically, someone came from the direction of that shed, possibly snuck up on him, and struck him with the brick."

9

———————

 donned a pair of gloves from the trunk of a cruiser. Catching Casey's gaze from a distance, I pointed to the shed, and she gave a sharp nod. The weathered wood groaned as I swung open the barn-style doors. Inside the dark space, I skimmed the walls in search of a light switch. Once my fingertips grazed over the upturned switch, I flicked it. Nothing. Flicking it a few more times didn't change the result.

I sighed, but it was only a minor setback. With my phone's flashlight on, I started to methodically sweep the space, first the right side, since most people were right-handed, and the habit of leaning to the right influenced almost every choice, from standing in line to where they stored items. If something, like the camera, was left in the shed, that's where I might find it.

Working my way to the back of the building, I moved empty cardboard boxes, half-filled bags of potting soil, rakes, and shovels. I brushed the back of my hand against my damp forehead, my fingers and palms sweaty inside the latex gloves. Along the far wall of the building, a workbench stretched the entire length, with shelves cluttered with paint cans and various handyman supplies. I shone the flashlight along a messy shelf, pausing when I saw that a box of screws had been moved: the dusty outline revealed the secret.

Snapping a few pictures, I spotted a step stool under the bench. I wanted a closer look. I wasn't going to disturb anything. There was no rule against looking if I didn't tamper with the evidence. I took in every small detail of the smudge of the dust trail, including the angle at which the box was now located. What was stashed behind it? My pulse quickened as I peered closer. While shining the flashlight down from the top, a protruding cylinder reflected the beam of light. Bingo!

I rushed to the entrance and called for Casey or the Sarge.

Josie strode to the shed. "Did you find a clue?"

I nodded, slipping her a quick wink. Before I could explain what, Casey ran over with Benson on her heels.

Her breath came in spurts. "Temperance, what's up?"

"See for yourself." I stepped aside.

Casey said, "Benson, grab flashlights."

"On it." He jogged to the cruiser.

Sarge strode over. "Casey, did Temperance uncover something?"

I gave him a satisfied smile. "Yes, I've found Adam's camera."

He frowned.

I said quickly, "Don't worry, I didn't touch a thing. I know the drill."

"Show me," he demanded.

I escorted Casey and Sarge to the back of the shed. Benson hurried forward and handed each of them a flashlight.

"When I was scanning the area, I noticed the dust around a box of screws had been smeared." I gestured to the stool. "Use that to get a better look."

The sergeant stood and leaned in. "Good work, Temperance." He got down. "Butler, have a look."

Benson handed her a pair of latex gloves, and she snapped

them on. Shining the flashlight beam, she took pictures, moved the box of screws, took more pictures, and said, "Well, hello. What do we have here?"

She glanced down. "Benson, we need two evidence bags."

My brow creased. "Two?"

"There's a film camera and some kind of cloth which looks like it has blood on it."

"How do you know the camera isn't digital?" I asked.

Casey pointed, "See the dials and levers on the top? That's all to adjust the camera's lens and the film winder."

"Interesting. If this is Adam's camera, I wonder why he was shooting film."

She shook her head. "Hard to say. The Poseys should have some insight."

Benson snapped open the first evidence bag. Casey documented the details by taking more pictures after she slid the camera into the bag. He then opened the second bag. Repeating the process, this time she withdrew a white cloth, a shirt with the inn's logo; the fabric was smeared with damp blood.

I let out a low whistle. This was a twist I hadn't seen coming. Not that I thought it was an employee who attacked Adam with a brick. The perpetrator had gotten close enough to get blood splatter on themselves and needed a way to get it off.

After Casey got down, she said, "Benson, secure the evidence and have the lab match the blood on the shirt to our victim, see if there are prints on the camera, and we'll need to ask Eunice where employees' shirts are stored."

"Yes, Ma'am."

"At the bakery, the original one, I had stacks of clean aprons and shirts for the employees in the back. I liked them to always look neat." I crossed to the left side of the room where two metal lockers stood, neither had locks on the handles. Tilting my head at them, I asked, "Wanna bet the shirts are stored in here?"

"You've got gloves on?" she asked.

I held up my hands. "Door number one *or* door number two?"

"Either. Both will be processed for prints and evidence."

I lifted the metal handle and eased open the door. Hanging neatly on a hook was a pair of suspenders, a yellow rain slicker, and a ball cap. Resting on the shelf, a coffee mug and an open pack of crackers.

"At first glance, nothing important in here." I closed the door and took a step to my left. The door was already ajar. Pulling it open, I sucked in a breath. Shelves lined the interior, one stacked with bottles of water and hand sanitizer, and another was a tidy pile of pale gray and white tees.

"Casey, the shirt may have come from here." I stepped back, giving her the full view.

She moved across the room and ran the beam of light down the locker to the concrete. "Look. Blood droplets on the floor."

Sergeant Franklin strode to the front of the building. His tone was clipped. "I need a team in here to process for evidence. Bring portable floodlights."

I snapped pictures. "Hypothetically, and based on what Max said, the brick was missing around two-fifteen this afternoon." I looked at my watch. "We found Adam at three and it's five. After Adam was struck, the attacker had blood on his hands. They tossed the brick, grabbed the camera, and ran in, hoping to find rags to wipe off the blood. What's better than a greasy rag? A clean shirt. Stashing everything, they got back outside, slipped into the inn, into a bathroom to finish cleaning up, and then back to the party."

Casey nodded. "Plausible. We need to search the inn for any blood."

This wasn't something Josie and I could help with, but I

was dying to do a walk-through of the inn. I said, "Casey, any chance?"

She held up her hand. "Not this time. If we find something, I'll share the pictures with you, but," taking a step closer to me, she lowered her voice, "there *is* something I need."

"Name it."

"Research. There's a lot of physical evidence to process, and I need to get a head start on understanding the possible reasons behind the crime. That's your forte. Dig up everything you can on our suspects, the family—heck, even Eunice —and the status of the inn."

"Sure. I'll text if I get any interesting hits on the suspects and victim." I scanned the shed one final time. "How did the attacker get out of here without being seen and slip into the inn to clean up?" Narrowing my eyes, I said, "I'm going to take one final look around, and I'll touch base later."

"Sounds like a plan. Thanks for your help, Temperance. It's good to have someone with your expertise on the team, and it doesn't hurt that I trust you." She gave me a tight smile and a half nod.

I exited the building, pulled off the latex gloves, and held up my hand to get Josie's attention, pointing to my SUV and the kitchen. She gave me a quick nod. I circled the shed before going to the kitchen door.

The little grassy area was tidy, too tidy, and not a place that guests would wander to. A drying rack stood with clothespins clipped in a neat row, and a hose was coiled neatly beside a green plastic watering can tipped on its side. A couple of weather-beaten Adirondack chairs shared a small table, with paint peeling from neglect. I frowned and walked closer. One bare wooden arm was darker than the other. That's odd. My stomach tightened as I moved closer. The arm was streaked with a rusty red color.

I zipped off a text to Casey, then knelt beside the watering can. Droplets of water lingered in the grooves.

"What have you found?"

Jumping at the sound of Casey's voice, I whirled around. She was so quiet I didn't hear her approach.

"Look—this is out of place." I gestured to the tipped can. "Everything here is neat and tidy, but the watering can is on its side." Crouching beside the chair, I pointed to the dark area on the armrest. "This could be where someone washed the blood off. The wood appears to be stained with a mixture of water and blood. Whoever used the can let it drip here."

"Good work." Casey rubbed her temples. "There's so much ground to cover and so many witnesses to talk to, it's been nearly impossible to investigate every area."

"Just trying to help. I know this gives you more work, but every instinct tells me this matters."

She gave a weary nod. "Agreed."

I snapped several pictures and stood. "I'm taking my things. Do you want to check the boxes first?"

She exhaled, shoulders sagging. "No. Just repack everything to make sure nothing was slipped into one of your boxes before you take off."

I patted her on the shoulder. "You've got this, Casey."

She met my gaze, her eyes fatigued. "I'm glad one of us is confident. A murder at a happy family event will scar everyone here."

There were no words to contradict the sentiment. My chin dipped as did my voice, "See you later."

Josie waited for me in the kitchen. My two totes were packed. "Hey, it seems like you uncovered a few clues?"

"Yeah, the camera, a blood-covered shirt, and potentially where the murderer cleaned up."

She gave a low whistle. "That's terrific. I didn't find a thing. However, I paid attention to several interesting conversations." Placing a finger over her lips, she said, "Later."

"Casey wants us to take off." I mimed typing on a keyboard. Who knew if someone was eavesdropping on our conversation? "Did you pack everything to make sure nothing was slipped in the boxes?"

"Yes, and I thought we could put the trays in Rob's car on our way out."

"We should." I lifted one tote, and Josie stacked the trays on it before she picked up the other one.

She looked around the room. The kitchen was cluttered with the caterer's stuff. "Who would have thought walking in here this morning that we'd be leaving like this?"

"Come on." I nodded to the interior swinging door. "Let's go out the front. We should find Cissy and Rob out there."

As we entered the main room, Cissy and Rob sat in wing-back chairs by a window overlooking a flower garden. We set the totes down and crossed the room.

Cissy looked up. Her eyes were bloodshot. Rob held her hand, as if they were clinging to a lifeline. "Temperance, I didn't realize you were still here."

"We've been cleared to leave and wanted to express how sorry we are for what happened."

Josie said, "Adam was a wonderful person, and I'm confident the police will arrest whoever did this."

Fresh tears welled up in her eyes. "Thank you, Josie, that's kind of you to say."

I pointed to the boxes. "We have your silver trays. Would you like us to put them in your car?"

Rob shook his head. "Don't worry about those today. It would be better if you came out to the house tomorrow, and I'd like to speak with both of you." He glanced over his shoulder. "Privately."

I nodded and said, "Is there a specific time?"

"Ten o'clock." It wasn't an ask or suggestion; he stated a time when he wanted us there.

Josie asked gently, "Is there anything we can do for you before we leave?"

Cissy stretched out her hand to Josie, clasping it tightly. "Be careful going home."

I reassured her, "We'll see you tomorrow." I withdrew a card from my pocket and handed it to Rob. "If you need anything, here's my contact information."

Rob slid it into his pocket without looking. "Thank you," his voice gruff.

I admired his strength to support his wife. "Have you seen Andrew?"

"Yes," Josie said, "He and Wendy are out speaking with some of the guests."

He frowned. "Is she working the crowd like she's the queen bee?"

Unsure how to answer it, I said, "She and Andrew are reassuring the guests they'll be able to leave soon."

"You're very diplomatic, Temperance. I appreciate your kindness." He kissed his wife's hand. "We'll see you at ten tomorrow."

"Certainly." I glanced at Josie, "Ready?" We retrieved the totes and left the building.

Silently, we loaded the items into my SUV. Andrew ran toward us, with dark sunglasses covering his eyes.

"Temperance, wait a moment."

I closed the hatch and paused. "Andrew."

"Are you taking the silver platters with you?"

"Yes. We saw your parents, and they asked us to keep them for safekeeping. With so much going on, they didn't want anything to happen to them."

A faint downturn of his lips would have been easy to miss if I hadn't been paying close attention. "Are you concerned?"

"Not really. I was going to offer to take them for you."

"That's not necessary, and I already reassured your father they'd be in good hands."

He clasped his hands in front of him. "Of course they are. Thank you for overseeing that detail. I'm sure you can understand that I don't want my mother dealing with any additional stress. If something happened to the family heirlooms? Well…it wouldn't be good."

"Your father has my card, and if he asks me to bring them out tonight, I will be happy to accommodate him. I, too, don't want to cause your family any additional stress." I put a strong emphasis on the word family to indicate where my loyalties lie.

He cleared his throat, glanced at the back of my vehicle, and said, "And it's appreciated." He extended his hand and gave mine a firm shake, then offered Josie a curt nod. "Drive carefully." With that he strode away.

I watched him rejoin Wendy and their group of friends. Curiously, he didn't take her hand or slip an arm around her waist.

"Josie, what do you make of that?"

"The fact he's worried about the family silver or the lack of affection toward his fiancée?"

"Both. They've suffered a terrible shock. Andrew's *twin* brother was murdered. From a behavioral standpoint, I'd expect raw grief or visible distress. Instead, he's focused on serving platters, ignoring the woman he's about to marry. That disconnect doesn't sit right with me."

Josie tilted her head. "It could be he's in shock. You know, people process trauma in their own way. Maybe latching onto the family silver is helping him avoid the reality of the situation."

I frowned. "Possible. But I'm keeping my eye on him."

I jingled the keys in my hand. "How's your brain processing all of this?"

"Muddled. You promised pizza and salad before we start to research. Is that still the plan?"

I gave her a tired smile. "The only lingering question: what do you want on it? I vote for meat lovers, with veggies and extra cheese."

10

———————

osie said, "It was too bad the wait for pizza was so long but grabbing burgers and shakes from the Bistro Shack was genius. And a smart move on Carter Edwards' part to open it up as a casual alternative to Bistro 9."

I eased into my drive and parked. "Exactly. After a day like ours, the last thing I'd want to do is shower and dress up just to eat, even if all I wanted was a pizza. This will hit the spot."

"Same. I needed something more substantial than Chinese takeout. And really—who doesn't love a thick milkshake? Besides, we need brain food."

"That's a true statement." I got out, opened the hatch, and slid out the silver trays. Josie already had the bag with our dinner. There wasn't anything else needed to come inside tonight. I shut the hatch and hit the lock button on the SUV.

A happy little bark reached my ears.

"Someone's about to be thrilled with his pup-burger," Josie laughed.

"Hank's reward for a long day." I climbed the front porch steps. Balancing the trays on my hip, I slipped the key in the lock. The door swung open. My fur baby ran toward me as fast as his short little legs would carry him, body and tail wiggling and showing off his sweet doxie smile.

I placed the trays on a table and dropped to my knees as he launched into my arms. "Hey Hank." I kissed the top of his velvety head. "Were you a good boy today?"

His sharp, happy bark was all I needed to hear as he covered my face and chin with puppy kisses.

Josie closed the door and went to the kitchen. She called over her shoulder, "Do you want to eat inside or on the deck?"

"The deck so Hank can spend some time outside." I put him down, and the little pup trotted after Josie.

I took several deep breaths, stretching my arms out in front of me and then overhead. This movement boosted my blood flow, and with so much information coming at me so quickly this afternoon, it gave me a moment to clear my mind.

After several more minutes, I entered the kitchen and put the trays on the sideboard. The sliding door was open, and Hank was cruising the fence line, his nose to the grass. Plates were on the counter and the containers were lined up. I put the extra burger we got in the refrigerator for Casey if she stopped by.

"Hank's burger is in his dish. I wasn't sure if you wanted to take it outside or have him eat in here."

"He can eat outside." I filled my plate, then paused to grab a pen and a notepad from the table. With a shrug, I tapped my brow. "I need to make organized chaos of this mess."

She nodded. "I get it, and I wish I'd been paying better attention to all the happenings around me. I might be able to help more."

I gave her a reassuring smile. "You remember more than you think, and as we talk, it will come back to you."

She chuckled, "I'm glad one of us is confident in my ability to recall events." She picked up her plate and milkshake. "Food first."

I laughed. "Agreed."

Hank looked up as we came out and then returned to sniffing.

"Temperance, what do you think he's hoping to find?"

"He has a high hunting drive, so who knows. But look at the top of the fence. There's a squirrel watching him. He knows the drill and won't come into the yard until Hank's safely inside."

She laughed. "Smart squirrel."

I bit into the burger and groaned as juice dribbled down my chin. "Oh-Em-Gee—this is ridiculously good." Even though my dinner was amazing, my thoughts turned to Adam and the nagging question of why someone would want him dead.

"Josie, everyone we talked with was adamant—Adam was well-liked."

She wiped her mouth and sipped her thick shake. "That's what they said. Do you think someone held a grudge?"

I arched a brow. "Like Ken Grayson? Would he be financially set with one of the twins eliminated?"

Her eyes widened. "I find that appalling, they're family."

"It's something I plan to ask Rob and Cissy about tomorrow when we take the trays back."

"What if Andrew and Wendy are there?"

My lips pressed into a hard line. "It makes sense they'd be at the house, but Wendy isn't exactly a beloved member of the Posey family. I suspect she'll keep her distance while trying to figure out how to keep the wedding on track."

Josie jerked back, her mouth gaped open. "You think she'll want to move ahead with the wedding as planned?"

I nodded. "I wouldn't put it past her. She didn't seem that broken up about Adam. Her real concern was for her party.

She didn't even try to console Andrew, from what I could see, and we both saw her chatting up the guests. It was like Rob said."

"I noticed," Josie frowned. "And what did she need to talk with Casey about that Andrew couldn't hear? Unless… you think she knows who wanted to attack Adam, and she was trying to protect Andrew from additional pain. Like if it was Ken? It's awful that Adam is dead, but if it was by his own family member," she shivered, "that would be worse."

"We need to stick to the facts." I wiped a blob of ketchup from my chin and placed my napkin on the empty plate. I picked up the pen and opened the notebook. "Before we left, Casey asked, well implied, if we could dig into everyone's background. We need to start with a list of suspects. I don't think we need to delve heavily into the guest list just yet. At this point, I don't have it, and for another reason, no one stands out as the guilty party."

JOSIE NODDED. "I agree. We need to begin with the people who have the most to gain from Adam's death, or Andrew's. It still could be a case of mistaken identity."

"I'm not ruling that out." I crossed my legs and held the pen poised to write. "Suspects are—Ken Grayson, Wendy Carmichael, Andrew Posey, Rob Posey, Cissy Posey, and Max Griffin…"

Josie lifted her hand, her eyes wide. "Wait. You're putting Rob and Cissy on the list? That's terrible."

"I'm not saying they killed their son. But they were at the scene and could have potential motives. We can't ignore them just because they're Adam's parents and are grieving. Everyone stays on the list until they can be cleared."

She sighed. "Then you'd better add Eunice Moss. Sweet or not, she should be on the list."

"Okay." I tapped the top of the pen to the paper. "What

about any friends of the family or catering staff? Did anyone stand out as acting suspicious or did you witness anyone arguing with Adam?"

She shook her head. "Every time I saw Adam, he was smiling, chatting with guests, and taking pictures. That camera was always in his hand."

"Same." Hank trotted over and head bumped my leg. I picked him up and set him on my lap. "What are the possible motives?"

"Besides money?" Tilting her head, Josie paused.

"Yes. The camera was tucked away. Was it that Adam took a picture of something he shouldn't have, and an argument broke out? It escalated quickly, and in the heat of the moment, someone picked up a brick and hit him? Before Josie could respond, I shook my head. "No— that doesn't feel right. This wasn't on impulse. It was deliberate. Sneaking into the shed and hiding the camera, that was planned. I'll bet whoever attacked never thought we'd search there."

"Where's your cell phone?" she asked. "I want to compare the platter to the art work Wendy sent me."

"Better yet, let's compare the art work to the actual platter."

We went inside and I placed Hank on the floor.

"Can I borrow your laptop and log into my email?" Josie asked.

I gestured to the computer on the counter. "Help yourself." Meanwhile, I placed the tray in the center of the kitchen table.

Josie tapped the keys. "Did you notice if the painting Wendy said needed to be hung near the buffet was there?"

"No, it wasn't." I frowned. "Which makes sense, I suppose, since the food tables were outside. There wasn't any place to hang it, but it's something we should ask Cissy about tomorrow."

I scribbled a note on a fresh piece of paper and underlined

it. Not that all questions wouldn't be important when we saw Rob and Cissy, but since it was the one detail that had been important to Wendy, it was troubling.

Josie carried the laptop to the table and set it down, screen open. "Here's the artwork Wendy emailed me. It was a low-res file, so I redrew it for printing purposes, but I followed it exactly."

I compared the crest on the screen to the one etched into the silver platter. My heart thudded. They were different.

"Josie, look— the book and rose detail above the crest isn't on the platter. I wish we had the painting to compare them. It would help in determining which one is wrong."

She leaned closer, squinting at the screen. "The more important question is why. What's so important about the book and the rose? And since this is a low-resolution file, was it something Wendy clumsily added herself, a personal twist on the family crest?"

"I don't think it's her way of trying to make her mark." I said slowly, "It feels intentional, a message for someone or it could be a foolish mistake, but to who and why?"

Josie leaned back in the chair, arms folded and said, "The rose makes sense, roses, flowers, Posey, it works. The floral connection works but the book." She shook her head, "That's an entirely different puzzle. Do you see a connection?"

I sat down and closed my eyes. "What does a book often signify in any type of symbol?"

Josie remained quiet as I rolled through ideas. When I looked at her, I said, "Here are a few possibilities. A religious book, like the Bible. Or perhaps detailed records of the family, such as deeds and genealogy, that sort of thing. Or even something linked to educational pursuits."

"Do we need to break them into separate items to research?"

I pursed my lips. "After we talk to Rob and Cissy, we will

have a better idea of which direction to take. For now, we can dig into the history of the Posey family crest."

Her brow arched and her eyes widened. "How?"

"There's a database for crests and coats of arms. If we compare versions that are published online, we might be able to tell if the change is historical or a more recent and possibly unauthorized change."

A grin tipped the corners of her mouth. "You've done this before, I'm guessing?"

I lifted a shoulder with a half-shrug. "Perhaps."

She slid the laptop to me. I saved a copy of the crest, logged out of her email, and dove into research mode.

"Any chance you can create a murder board for us?" I asked after a few minutes, glancing up from the screen. "Create a dedicated page for the crest information. I'll print copies of the pictures I took of the tray and your logo. If you can add them to the board, that will help for quick reference."

"Send them to print." She hurried into my office as I tapped the keys for both sets of images.

I called over my shoulder, "The easel and paper pads are in the office closet."

What I didn't add was that I bought these just in case we ever found ourselves tangled up in another one of Casey's investigations. I usually worked better with dry-erase boards where I could see the notes spread out in front of me. However, this was better since the pad was like a giant sticky note; we could tear off the pages and plaster the walls with clues or timelines if needed.

"Hey, this pad is neat." She set up the easel and smoothed the top page into place. "I even grabbed colored markers since it might be useful to color-code our notes."

My brow cocked as I fought to suppress a grin. "Careful, Josie, you're starting to sound like you're going full detective mode."

She gave me a mock, but serious nod. "I know, right? The

next thing I know, I'll be ordering push pins and red string like I've seen on TV."

I laughed. "Let's solve this one before you start redecorating my walls like an episode of 'The Cozy Nook Bookstore.'"

She smirked. "The big difference there, we're not witches with a talking familiar." She petted Hank's head. "But if Hank could speak, we'd really be in business."

I laughed. "Or in serious trouble. Can you imagine him demanding even more treats?" Peering closer to the screen I said, "Bingo."

"Did you find something?" She dragged a chair close to me and sat.

I turned the screen so she could see it. "Here it is, a slide show of the evolution, or lack thereof, for the Posey family crest." I tapped the first image. "This one shows it was awarded to the family in the late seventeenth century to Sir William Posey for his service to the Crown during a border conflict. Pretty standard with the floral motif and shield." I clicked forward. "Now here, the crest changes in the late 1800s after the family emigrated to the States when the rose was added, but the book doesn't appear until almost a century later." I pointed to the next image, giving Josie time to examine the drawings.

Her eyes widened. "That was less than one hundred years ago, and after they settled here."

I nodded, my stomach tightening. "I'm going to take a leap and say the book isn't decorative. Whatever it represents has been discovered or will be soon. And, I'd bet my bakery cart it's connected to something either Rob and Cissy don't want discovered or they don't know about it and Andrew and Wendy do."

"Maybe Ken too," Josie said.

I looked up from my computer. My heart was heavy in my chest. "And maybe Adam died to protect the secret."

11

─────────

$\mathcal{A}$t five till ten, I drove down the long, winding drive to the Posey compound.

Josie sat silently in the passenger seat, her hands clasped in her lap, her face drawn.

I peered out the windshield. "The dark clouds appear to be in mourning; it suits the day."

Josie's voice was so soft I had to strain to hear her. "Less than forty-eight hours ago, Adam carried fancy silver trays to your SUV. Now, he's dead. Murdered."

I reached across the console and clasped her hand, squeezing. "Stuff like this is never easy."

When we arrived yesterday, Cissy greeted us with a friendly wave from the steps. Today, there was a heavy silence as I slowed down. A dark green Range Rover was in the space I had used the other day. I pulled in beside it and parked. Turning in my seat, I said, "I can do this alone if you don't want to go in."

She shook her head firmly, her eyes fixed on the house. "Not a chance. Adam was a good guy and deserves both of us doing everything we can to find out who did this, get justice for him, and for the family too."

I gave her hand one last reassuring squeeze. "Then let's do this." Pushing open the driver's door, I popped the hatch. By the time I got to the back, Josie was already pulling the trays out. I took half and we climbed the front steps side by side. Her jaw was set, her determination matching mine.

Moments like this reminded me why I had joined the Bureau to tip the scales of justice one case at a time. Yet there was one case which remained unsolved. He haunted my dreams; it was his anguish I felt in the middle of the night, begging me to bring him home so he could finally rest in peace.

Josie grabbed my arm, her eyes clouded with worry. "Temperance, what's wrong?"

I forced myself to exhale and shook my head, pushing away the memories. "I'm, I'm okay…an echo from the past. Nothing more."

She held on. "Maybe I can help."

"I wish you could." A sad smile tugged the corners of my lips. "But thank you."

The front door opened. Rob Posey stood in the doorway, dressed casually and barefoot. In an instant, his world shifted. He no longer appeared as the head of a powerful family; he was simply a father carrying his grief with every breath. He didn't speak, only watched silently as we made our way up the walk.

"Ladies, thank you for bringing the platters." He stepped away from the door. "Please come in. Cissy's waiting in the living room."

"Of course. Where should we put the trays?" I looked around at the highly polished surfaces. I was hesitant to set them down.

He held out his hands, his eyes devoid of emotion. "I'll take them." He gestured to the archway. "Through there. I'll be in momentarily."

We entered the spacious living room. It was large but

somehow felt cozy. With several seating areas, a silent grand piano occupied one corner. I wondered whose fingers had touched the keys and if the joy would come back so they could play again. At the other end of the room, near a set of French doors opening to a slate patio, stood Cissy.

As we approached, I noticed her eyes were red-rimmed and puffy from hours of crying. I gently hugged her. "I'm so sorry for your loss." Yesterday had been a blur, and I wasn't sure if I'd expressed my regrets properly.

Then Josie hugged her tight. "Cissy, there are no words…"

She nodded and gave us a weak smile. "Thank you for coming over this morning. I'm sure it was the last thing you wanted to do."

"Nonsense," I said softly. "We're glad to be here." I didn't add that I had questions; those would come later. For now, it was about easing this poor woman's grief if that was even possible.

She waved her hand to the sofa behind us. "Please, have a seat. I made tea."

Josie and I waited until she sat down on the loveseat; she seemed to have aged ten years since we last saw her. Her hand trembled as she poured four cups and handed one to us. Rob entered from the patio, pressed a kiss to her cheek, and then sat next to her.

I met Rob's gaze. "Are Andrew and Wendy joining us?"

His lips thinned, his tone flat. "Not right now. They have things to take care of at the inn."

"Oh." I brought the cup to my lips. "The tea is delicious."

"Thank you. I order it from a small family-owned business in Pine Valley, Maine—MRM Teas."

She sipped, and Rob slid his arm around her shoulders. Giving his wife a worried look, he nodded. "Temperance, I'd like to hire you to find out who killed Adam."

I carefully set the dainty tea cup on the table. "Rob. I'm

flattered, but I'm not in the investigative business anymore. The police will find out who did this."

Cissy shook her head. "No. We need you. It's not that the police aren't capable, but they have to stick to the rulebook. You don't. And you too, Josie." She focused on Josie. "We need both of you."

"Cissy, I'm—we're flattered." I slid forward. "But we're not…"

Rob held up his hand. "I know about your reputation with the Bureau and your contribution to the investigations for the bakery fire and the death of Franny Clark. There's no need to be modest. You and Josie see what others miss or overlook as trivial, and you have an uncanny knack for finding the truth."

Even though Casey had requested our help, having Rob and Cissy ask was a different matter. If we agreed, would they share everything they knew? I glanced at Josie and then back at Rob.

"Before we commit, I have a few questions. Depending on what you can tell me, we'll see what happens next."

Cissy grasped Rob's hand, her chin trembled, but she gave a determined nod. "Ask anything. We have no secrets from each other."

"All right. But first, we must agree that the conversation we're about to have stays between the four of us."

"But Andrew—" Her voice wavered.

I shook my head gently. "I don't mean to sound harsh, given the circumstances, but until we know who's responsible, we have to keep this circle small. Whatever Andrew knows, he would most likely share it with Wendy and possibly Ken. We can't risk that."

Rob's jaw clenched, his eyes hard. "Do you suspect them?"

I looked him in the eye and didn't flinch, "For now, everyone's a suspect, including you and Cissy."

He swallowed hard before meeting my gaze. "Fair enough. We won't say a word."

Cissy did a zipper motion over her lips. "Sealed."

"Do you know why Adam might have been a target?" I asked. It was a difficult question for the grieving couple, but necessary.

Cissy shook her head. "No. Rob and I have racked our brains, and nothing stands out. Adam was happy to be home, but was equally as happy to leave in a few months. He's working on some new photography, and that's been his happy place since he was a kid."

Josie asked, "He never had any interest in the family business?"

Rob said, "No. In fact, I run his photography business, and a lawyer friend of the family handles his contracts with the gallery. Adam jokes..." he pressed his fingers to his eyes and Cissy leaned into him, "joked he didn't inherit a film canister full of my business acumen."

Cissy's voice softened, "He loved using an old Canon and thirty-five-millimeter film for black and white shots. It wasn't how he made a living—it was how he expressed himself. He used to joke that black and white images allowed him to breathe in the work and exhale unflinching honesty, the soul of a single moment captured forever."

I asked. "Hasn't film become passé? With advances in digital, the quality is extraordinary."

Rob's sorrow-filled smile was faint. "That's true, but I've listened to Adam a thousand times talk about the art of shooting with film. It wasn't something that could be rushed. The shutter captured true light and shadow; it wasn't enhanced or altered, unlike digital images. Shooting with film had a simplicity that reflected talent. Not that he was comparing himself to his idol, Ansel Adams—but his photos moved people."

That cleared up one mystery, almost. "Do you know what camera he was using yesterday?"

Cissy's brow creased. "He always had the film and digital cameras with him. Weren't they found?"

"To my knowledge, only the film camera has been recovered," I said.

She sat up straighter. Her words were laced with panic. "Can we have it back?"

Josie leaned forward. "I'm sure it will be returned to you once the investigation is complete."

Cissy's hands twisted in her lap, her voice held a sob. "Rob, you have to talk to the police. I want a professional handling that film. Those photos—his last—can't be lost. It's all we have left of him."

I slid from where I was to sit next to Cissy. Placing my hand over hers, I said, "I promise you: Officer Butler won't let anything happen to the camera or the film and they *will* be returned to you."

She gripped my arm, and her voice cracked. "Won't they need to see the pictures? What if Adam snapped a photo of something or someone who wanted it kept a secret?"

"I'm sure that's an avenue they'll explore. If it will put your mind at ease, Rob should contact Casey to make sure the film will be processed carefully."

"Good idea." He stood and strode across the room, picked up a cell phone, and came back. "She might have an expert she can work with. Better yet, I'll fly someone I know out here at my expense."

He dialed before I could ask who he was talking about.

"Pad? Rob Posey here." He paused.

"That's why I'm calling. I have bad news."

He nodded and bit the corner of his lip.

"Adam was attacked yesterday and died at Andrew's engagement party."

Cissy clung to me. Tears slid down her cheeks.

"Thank you, but I'm calling to ask a favor—not just as Adam's friend, but as a police officer."

That was the connection I'd been missing. A trusted friend of the family, law enforcement professional, but I wasn't sure about the photographer angle.

"Adam was using his SLR, the film version. The police have the camera but we want to make sure the images are preserved. As a photographer, could you come to Oak Hollow and develop the film? I'll pave the way with the local department."

He paused. His chin dipped, as did his voice. "Thank you, Pad. I'll be in touch shortly with your flight details. You'll stay with us at the house; there's plenty of room."

He nodded again. "Thank you."

His eyes met mine. "I'll call Officer Butler next. Is that your only question?"

I kept my voice even. "No. Who is this person?"

Rob never flinched under my slight challenge. "Padraic Stone. He's a well-known photographer and a police officer."

The cogs of the wheels in my brain all clicked together. A well-known photographer and cop…he sounded like a dream resource. If Rob wanted him here, Stone must be good.

Josie quirked a brow and gave a slight nod, and I returned the gesture. It was apparent she'd heard of him, too. I wanted to know about the changes to the crest.

Rob paced the length of the living room with the phone pressed to his ear. Over the next ten minutes, he spoke with Sergeant Franklin, who approved Pad Stone as an expert. Then Rob arranged for a private jet to fly to Loudon and pick him up. When he finally sank to the couch, his shoulders sagged, and his head tipped back against the cushions.

Cissy said, "Hon, calling Pad was a good idea."

His gaze softened as it rested on his wife. When it shifted to me, it turned sharp as steel. "I'll do whatever it takes to put the guilty person behind bars. No matter who it is."

The message was crystal clear. He wasn't pulling any punches; the gloves were off and he was ready to fight for justice.

I nodded, appreciating his sentiment.

Waiting for a moment, he asked, "What else do you need to know?"

"Josie, do you have the printout of the invitation?"

Cissy's brows knit together. "The wedding invitation? I hardly see how that's relevant to Adam's death." The way she reacted yesterday was something to take note of.

"Maybe it's nothing," I said evenly, "but as I've said, I have questions."

Rob raked a hand through his short blond hair, his expression weary. "Go ahead. We're ready."

Taking his hand, Cissy nodded. "Anything to help."

Josie withdrew the invitation from her shoulder bag and passed it to me along with a print of the photo I had taken of the silver tray.

Placing them side by side, I held out the image of the tray. "Yesterday, when I was cleaning the trays, I noticed something odd. At the time, I couldn't quite put my finger on it. It wasn't until later, when I saw the invitation again, that I realized what it was." I handed them the cardstock. "As you can see on the tray, the crest matches the design from the late seventeenth century. However, there is a record of a change in the early twentieth century when the book and rose were added."

Rob studied the pages and said, "Where did you get the file with the book and rose?"

Josie frowned. "Wendy forwarded it to me to use on the invitations. I assumed she got it from you."

His face flushed red as he shook his head sharply. "Never. I don't use the new crest; I only use the original. I would never have sent this to her to insert on the wedding invitation." He looked at Cissy. "Do you have any ideas?"

Cissy stared at the papers and took the invite, her trembling fingertips tracing the book and rose as if she expected them to reveal a secret. Beside her, Rob's jaw jutted; he held tension in his face like he was trying not to say something. The altered crest loomed, silent but powerful.

Finally, she looked from Josie to me. "Rob, Josie showed me this yesterday but I was so angry I went to confront Wendy but when I didn't find her, I found Adam." She choked back a sob. "Where did Wendy say she got this?"

Josie frowned, "She didn't. It was attached to an email for the invitation."

I looked between Rob and Cissy. "What is it about this version that has you upset?"

He shook his head. "Nothing. Not really. Just a made-up story, best to be ignored."

I tented my fingers and leaned forward. "I can't do that, Rob. This could be connected to Adam's death. Either you can tell me, or I'll dig and uncover the truth. It's in your best interest to save me the time and trouble and give me the details."

A heavy silence settled over us. I didn't move. Across from me, Josie sat rigid, tension rolling off her in waves. The antique grandfather clock kept time with my pulse, each pendulum swing echoing a steady countdown.

12

——————

"You're right." Rob gave a slight nod, his voice low but unwavering. "Cissy, we're asking Temperance and Josie to help us. We must be completely transparent."

She nodded, folded her hands in her lap, and said, "When Rob's great-great-grandfather inherited the estate, his younger brother was furious, stating that since he was married and had a male heir, he should inherit. It was messy business, but the will was iron-clad. The brother received a small portion of the inheritance and vowed to take his revenge on losing control of Rose Hill."

My eyes narrowed. "What's Rose Hill?"

Josie nodded. "Is it a piece of land in town?"

Rob said, "Well, that's part of the bigger question. There are no records available on the location of Rose Hill. We believe it's located in Oak Hollow, but we've never found actual proof. What kind of real estate developers would we be if we couldn't find our own land? When my grandad took over the company, he reverted to the original crest, thus hiding the existence of the book and rose. We think the rose represents the land, and the book is a ledger with the details."

Josie said, "The rose represents Posey land, and the details are sealed in a book."

Cissy said, "Something like that. Over the years, we've tried to find it, but we've been unable to locate the book. And trust me, I've searched the library, but there are thousands of books in there."

"Have you searched the *entire* library?" I asked.

She shuddered. "Heavens no. When we first got married, I made an effort. Rob and I knew we wanted to protect our future children's legacy. But then I had children to raise and charity work I was passionate about. There was no time and the last thing I wanted or needed to do was be tethered to that room with all those ancient books."

Rob said, "Over the years, we've pushed it aside. Which is why hearing and seeing that Wendy must have discovered this crest and chose to use it on her invitations is distressing. Why would she use that version? She must have uncovered the truth and is trying to expose it. But, for what gain? She's a realtor and understands the value of land. In a few weeks, this family will be her family, and she should want to protect *her* children's future."

Cissy cried, "What if she's after more than marrying Andrew and is trying to swindle something out from under our noses? And Adam was killed thinking it was Andrew— and it's my fault for not listening to Adam when he said there was something fishy about that girl." Tears sprang to her eyes. "Even Eunice let it slip that Wendy wasn't a good match for Andrew."

The mistaken identity was one idea I'd had. "Cissy, I'm not sure if that's the case. If it were Wendy, wouldn't she have waited until after the wedding before she tried to harm Andrew?"

Rob's eyes narrowed. "Or worse—after he had redrawn his will!"

"Wait. Eunice mentioned Wendy?" My voice came out

sharper than I intended. Something about Eunice being involved in this mess didn't make sense.

Dabbing her damp eyes with a hanky, she nodded. "Yes, I've lent Eunice books from our library for years; she's a history buff, and a couple of weeks ago she stopped by to return one. We were reviewing last-minute details for the engagement party, and she let it slip. Of course, she apologized profusely. I'm sure she didn't want to offend me and risk ending my history of hosting events at the inn. I try to steer as much business her way as I can since she's struggled after her husband passed away."

"That's very nice of you. Not everyone would help Eunice like you have."

"We've known her for years." Rob said, "She's been desperate to get more large party bookings at the inn. The engagement party and wedding guests are a boost, but she needs it to be a regular occurrence to keep her business in the black."

This was a lot for me to process. Eunice was closely tied to the family. Could she have stumbled across something in one of the books and dangled it in front of Wendy, hoping to establish a quid pro quo relationship? A Posey family secret in exchange for a steady stream of bookings at her inn when Wendy's friends came to visit. But a parcel of land no one had heard about? It was highly likely Rose Hill was a real location. It could be another clue, rather than the actual name of a plot of land. "Could she have discovered the secret about Rose Hill?" I asked.

Cissy glanced at me. "Wendy or Eunice?"

"Wendy, of course. Eunice might be the town busybody, but she's been a loyal friend." Rob sighed.

"So we're back to Wendy discovering the secret. Did she spend time alone in the library?" Josie asked.

Cissy shrugged. "She might have. Over the last month or

so, she's been moving her clothes and other personal items into the north wing where she and Andrew will live."

I couldn't help but wonder if I heard a slight edge to the older woman's tone; her face was a blank canvas, revealing nothing. "You've never seen her in the library?"

"No." This time her tone was frosty.

Rob arched his brow and frowned. "We may not like the girl, but that doesn't mean she's a cold-blooded killer."

"I guess you'll figure out that I'm not a Wendy fan. I think Andrew could have done much better, but as soon as they started dating and he brought her home, all I saw were dollar signs in her green eyes." Cissy gave Rob a piercing look. "My husband feels the same, but we put our suspicions aside for Andrew. Now I'm second-guessing myself. If we had been more vocal about her, maybe Adam would be alive."

I said, "Cissy. Rob. It's easy to point the finger of guilt at Wendy in this moment. We must be logical, and again, I impress upon you to keep this conversation between the four of us."

Cissy faced Josie and asked, "Josie, what's your impression of my son's fiancée?"

Shifting in her seat, she said, "It's hard to say. I don't know her beyond the few interactions I've had while designing the invitation. She hasn't been the easiest customer to work with, but I've put it down as wedding jitters. Getting married and wanting everything to be perfect is a lot of pressure."

That was a very diplomatic answer, and inwardly, I was proud of Josie, and I'd tell her so later.

She continued, "Although I was surprised she didn't ask to have the crest on the invitation from the beginning of our conversations."

"I didn't expect that she'd ignore Rob's requests; he's had so few for this wedding, and he wanted the crest." Cissy exhaled and leaned against the cushions. "But the original."

I wasn't sure if she was starting to appear more relaxed because she trusted us to help, or was turning the conversation toward Wendy, making it easier for her not to focus on Adam's murder.

Rob leveled his gaze. "Temperance, you've asked a lot of questions but you never answered mine."

"That's fair. You might have guessed by my questions that this situation is quite complex, and the police asked me to consult on a few things. I'd like to explore the crest angle, with your permission, of course. Josie and I will need access to your library, and I promise, we'll be discreet. You have many things that will need your attention." I didn't want to have to use the word funeral.

Rob took Cissy's hand. "Thank you. When do you want to get started?"

I gave them a gentle smile. "We already have."

Rob and Cissy stood on the steps, arms wrapped around each other's waist, and watched as I drove away from the stately home.

Josie said, "I feel so bad for them. Losing a son, discovering their future daughter-in-law might be the reason why, and Andrew doesn't have any idea about her either."

Pulling my attention from the road, I glanced at her. "Do you think Andrew's oblivious? Even if Wendy isn't guilty of the worst, deliberately using a family crest that wasn't public knowledge is thumbing her nose at the family; it's disrespectful. It's possible she was trying to signal someone about what she discovered—someone on the guest list." I tightened my grip on the steering wheel. "We need to return to the Posey house tomorrow and search the library. Can you ask Cissy for the guest list?"

Josie smirked. "No need. I have it. Once the invitations

came back, I was supposed to print out return address labels for the response card envelopes."

"I thought they were going to a calligrapher?"

"To be addressed, yes. However, the Carmichael return address was printed on the main invitation envelope, but each RSVP received a pre-printed label, which I offered to do."

"How fortuitous." I grew quiet. "You've never heard of Rose Hill?"

She shook her head. "No. We'll need to search town records and the registry of deeds, but that database is based on name and address. I'm not sure it will be very helpful."

"Has Eunice lived in Oak Hollow for a long time?"

Josie said, "As far as I know, she was born here, and her husband's family opened the inn." She looked at me. "What are you thinking?"

"We need to take a detour. I want to check on Eunice, see how she's doing, ask her about the Posey library, and get her impressions of Wendy and her relationship with the guests staying at the inn."

Josie smiled, "I see. Like if she was particularly cozy with someone besides Ken?"

"Yes, and since Eunice has borrowed half of the Posey library over the years, maybe she came across a reference to Rose Hill or saw the other crest."

Josie pointed to a road sign ahead on the right. "Take the next road, it'll cut about ten minutes off the drive to the inn."

I clicked on my blinker, "I'm glad you're the co-pilot on this adventure."

Her smile dimmed. "I wish we didn't have a new quest."

I nodded and said softly, "A quest for a crest."

After making the turn, the road narrowed to little more than one lane. I slowed down to take the sharp turns carefully.

Josie screamed and grabbed the door handle, "LOOK OUT!"

I swerved to the right as a dark SUV roared past us, taking their lane out of the middle. I skidded to a stop, branches scraping the passenger side, the seatbelt digging into my shoulder. Unbuckling, I threw open the driver's door and jumped out, trying to get the license plate number, but I wasn't quick enough; the vehicle disappeared in a cloud of dust.

The faint smell of burnt tire rubber and pine needles scented the air. Leaning into the open driver's door, I asked, "Josie, are you all right?"

She nodded, her eyes wide. "Did you see who it was?"

I looked over my shoulder at where the SUV had gone, wondering if they would come back to check on us. But the only sound I heard was birds chirping and the wind rustling in the tree canopy.

"I hope that was just an irresponsible driver..." *and it wasn't someone looking to stop us from asking questions.*

"We should hurry to the inn. Maybe someone attacked Eunice."

"Agreed. I'm going to ease the car back onto the road and check the tires, just to be safe. We don't need to have a blow out."

I slid behind the wheel and dropped the SUV into low so that we'd gain traction in the underbrush to get out. At first, there was resistance. We were really tangled in the underbrush. I continued to apply steady pressure to the gas pedal, and finally, whatever was holding us broke free. Once on the road, Josie and I got out, walked around the vehicle, and inspected the tires. Other than paint scratches, it was in fine shape.

"We need to go," she said, "If anything's happened to Eunice, the cops will be back at the inn. She's already worried about keeping her business open; another incident will only make things harder for her."

I pressed my lips together. Eunice was worried about her inn, and Max was focused on future business. What was Adam's killer so desperate to hide? Maybe something he saw, or worse, took photos of? As I drove the last few miles, a chill slid down my spine. Where was the other camera? If Rob and Cissy were correct, in addition to the film version, Adam had the digital camera with him at the party. Could the killer have taken it? I pressed down the accelerator. *And if Adam's digital camera was in the killer's hands, they could erase the truth forever.* My stomach twisted into a hard knot. The murder was about silencing Adam, but the photos held the final story; without them, no one would ever know the truth. *For a town built on its image, there's a lot of turmoil bubbling under the surface.*

I turned into the inn's driveway and slammed on the brakes, narrowly missing a cameraman and reporter. The parking area overflowed with news vans, and people swarmed the grounds like ants at a picnic.

"Josie," I whispered, "do you think Eunice is holding a press conference?"

She pulled her sunglasses down her nose and looked over the top. "If she is, the inn will be booked solid for months."

13

We got out, and I locked my car. Scanning the crowd, my heart sank. There was Eunice standing on the top porch steps, hands raised like a conductor, waiting for the orchestra to quiet down and focus on her.

"Everyone. Please." Her voice carried over the gaggle of reporters. "I'll answer all your questions, but we must have some sense of order. I can't possibly answer properly if you're all shouting at once."

Under my breath, I uttered, "Just great." I grabbed Josie's hand, "Let's derail this debacle."

Pushing my way through with a wave of excuse me and pardon me, I finally reached the steps. I choked back what I wanted to say. *So much for her grieving Adam; she's grandstanding and relishing all the attention.*

Through gritted teeth, I nodded to the door. "Eunice, can we speak to you inside?"

"Temperance, can it wait?" She glanced over the crowd, and a smile tugged at the corners of her lips. "The reporters are waiting for a statement."

"They can keep waiting." I took her arm and steered her

into the inn. Josie shut the door and flipped the lock. "Temp, should I call Casey?"

"Yes. Tell her we need the scene cleared, and a few officers will need to stay and make sure no one else is granted an impromptu interview or unauthorized access."

Josie held her phone to her ear and turned her back to me.

"Eunice, why don't you sit down and tell me what you were doing out there?" I shook my head. "Talking to the press is a terrible idea, especially while this is an active investigation."

She dipped her chin. "I'm sorry. I hadn't thought it would do any harm. The reporters never went around back. I made sure they all knew what area was off limits."

Like they'd listen. I slapped my hand to my forehead. "Eunice, I understand that you own the inn, and you need to reassure any potential guests that the inn is safe. But Adam was killed less than twenty-four hours ago. Don't you think it's tone deaf to Rob and Cissy that you're planning your comeback?"

Eunice said, "This inn is like the town of Oak Hollow; reputation is everything. Once it's tarnished, you can't ever make it shine again. If I don't fight to protect it, I stand to lose everything. I already lost Fred."

Her grief-soaked words tugged at my soft underside. However, there was something about her statement that seemed almost…too polished. Had she rehearsed it for her press conference? I tipped my head and studied her. She shifted on the sofa and stared out the window at the restless crowd.

"Are you sure I couldn't just say a few words? To reassure folks the inn is safe and to let everyone know the police will find who hurt Adam?"

"Adam was murdered." Why did she continue to downplay what had happened to him? Could she still be in shock, and this was the way she was protecting herself?

"Temperance, you don't need to sound harsh. I know the poor man died right behind my inn." She shuddered, "Forgive me for not using the M-word. Do you think I need you to remind me?"

I wasn't sure since Eunice seemed almost glib about the current events, and my gut pinged like someone was evading the truth. *It must be the shock.*

Josie turned. "Casey said officers are en route and to stay inside until she gets here." She turned to Eunice and gave her a sympathetic smile. "Officer Butler understands why you'd want to reassure potential guests that the inn is safe, but there's a risk you could inadvertently slip and say something that could slow the investigation."

"You're right, Josie, and I'm sorry, Temperance. I wasn't thinking about the big picture. I've been so concerned about keeping my head above water, I've been in fight mode a long time."

"Since Fred passed, of course," I murmured as I patted her shoulder.

Josie gave me a quizzical look, one laced with a silent question. Whatever was on her mind, we'd circle back to later.

"Have all the guests from the party checked out?" I tilted my head, keeping my voice soft to put the older woman at ease.

She nodded. "They left either last night or very early this morning. Of course, that was after Casey cleared everyone."

"You're here alone?" Josie asked.

Her gaze darted from Josie to me. "No. Wendy—she's a sweet girl—stayed over last night. You know, just until things calmed down a bit."

"Where's Andrew?" I was curious how she'd react to a simple question.

"Andrew?" Eunice's mouth almost formed a smile. "He went for a drive, said he needed to clear his head."

I leaned closer to Eunice. "Did Wendy go with him?"

She frowned. "Now that you ask, no. She's still upstairs. He came down and got her a carafe of coffee and a plate of your delicious coffee cake. Then I heard raised voices, but I couldn't make out what they were saying. Right after, a door slammed, and he stormed out of here, peeling out of the driveway, kicking up stones. I thought it was strange, but you know, with the reporters here, I didn't have time to check on Wendy."

My heart quickened. "What car did he leave in?"

"A dark green SUV. You know, with tinted windows and huge tires."

A dark SUV. Oversized tires. Tinted windows. That sounded like the SUV that ran us off the road and had been at the Posey house when we arrived. Josie started to speak, but the words died on her lips. Instead, she arched her brows and tipped her head. Her expression said more than words could have; she made the connection, too.

"Wendy's still upstairs?" Josie gave the curved staircase a nod.

Eunice stood. "I would assume so. I didn't see her leave. I'll get her."

I reached out and touched her arm. "No need. Let's just relax for a few minutes. So much has happened, I'm sure you could use a moment or two."

Josie sat in a chair opposite the sofa. Eunice's gaze flicked to the stairwell, chewing the corner of her lower lip, she finally sat down on the edge of the sofa.

"We returned the silver trays to Cissy earlier and she mentioned that you're an avid reader."

Josie gave a half nod. As if to say let the questioning begin.

Eunice smiled. "I love history and their personal library is chock full of historical accounts on almost every subject— England, the Posey family arrival in the United States, the town, different wars in Europe, and our wonderful town." She clasped her hands. "Did you know the family crest was awarded to one of Rob's ancestors during the border war in Europe, for his service to the Crown? Imagine being able to boast that your family did something that important?"

Josie shot me a quick look, her eyes widened briefly as if to say Eunice might be a bit too invested in the Posey's past. Or was that me projecting?

"It's fascinating. What's the most interesting thing you've discovered?" I asked.

Eunice narrowed her eyes and tapped her chin with her index finger. "That's hard to say. Every book is a treasure trove of interesting tidbits."

I knew I couldn't push her; the ideas needed to roll around in her memory. Maybe, just maybe, it was too much to hope she'd say something more about the family crest.

A kerfuffle outside drew my attention. Dang it. I didn't need an interruption now. I crossed the room, drew back the lace curtain, and looked outside. With a glance over my shoulder, I said, "Reinforcements have arrived."

Someone gave the door a sharp rap, followed by Casey calling to me. I hurried across the room and unlocked the door.

"Come in. We thought it best to keep the door locked."

Casey gave me a brisk nod. "Good thinking." Her gaze swept the room and she nodded to Josie and Eunice.

"Josie, thanks for calling this in. You were right to be concerned about Eunice speaking to the press."

Eunice stated, "I've done nothing wrong. Those people were on my property, and all I wanted to do was convey that this was a respectable place to stay. What's the big deal? Temperance and Josie made me feel like I was giving away top-secret information."

Ah, Eunice was doing the classic deflection tactic. Trying to make it appear that Josie and I had done something inappropriate rather than Eunice being out of line by speaking to reporters. I wasn't worried. I'd stand by what I did, and I'd do it again.

Josie said, "Casey, thanks for coming out. What do you need us to do?"

"Eunice, would you mind waiting here for a moment while I speak with Temperance and Josie in the other room?"

She threw her hands up. "Sure, why not keep me in the dark about this investigation that pertains to me and my inn?"

I didn't appreciate the sarcasm that dripped from her words.

Casey said, "It's not about leaving you out. The police department needs their help. I'm sure you understand this is an active investigation and these ladies have a way of finding clues that might not be apparent to the trained eye. Their skepticism is an asset, and I'm sure you can appreciate me wanting to use everyone I have available to me to solve Adam's murder."

Eunice pressed her lips into a thin line as she flinched at the word murder. "Fine, but I don't like being left out."

"Understood." Casey ushered us into a small sitting room. She closed the door, paused, then cracked it open and shifted her body so that she had a clear view to the hallway and main room.

Smart. This way, Casey could monitor if anyone came into the room or if Eunice tried to leave.

"What can we do?" I asked.

"The uniformed officers will corral the reporters and, with luck, get them to leave, stating there will be no statement today. While that's happening, could you and Josie take another walk around the grounds, including the tent area? There's a digital camera missing and we need to find it."

I nodded, glancing at Josie. "We wondered if it was in police custody."

Josie said, "Is there someplace specific where we should concentrate our search?"

Casey shook her head. "I wish I could give you some direction. My team has scoured the entire area and come up with nothing. It has to be here. According to all witnesses' accounts, Adam had two cameras with him throughout the day. We only have the one you found in the shed. I'm hoping lightning will strike twice and you'll find it."

"Oh, did Rob Posey bring you up to speed? He's sent a plane to Loudon to bring back Padraic Stone."

Before I could go expand, she said, "Do you know who he is?"

"A world-famous photographer, and Rob mentioned he's a cop."

"Yeah, and his aunt is Winifred Simpson."

Now it was my turn to be surprised. I blinked hard. Even I had heard of her—she wasn't just famous—she was legendary.

Josie let out a low whistle. "That's his aunt. Talent must run in their DNA, and he's quite the package."

Casey nodded. "You'll like him. Which is why I'd like to find that other camera—so Pad can review those images too. It will be critical if someone tries to destroy the memory card; he might be able to recover it."

I nodded. "Makes sense. Did you let the team know we'll be poking around?" If Pad Stone could process the film and analyze the digital images, we might have a chance to wrap this case up quickly. It was the only gift we could give to Rob and Cissy, and possibly let them breathe again.

I said, "In addition to Adam's camera, you should know that Wendy used an obscure version of the Posey family crest on the invitations. There's a book and a rose sealed in wax at the top. We haven't had a chance to research it yet, but Rob didn't give Wendy access to that version, and he's unsure how she got her hands on it. He was upset when Josie showed them the invitation. My gut's saying Wendy's up to something."

Josie said, "I don't think it was a decorative touch for the invitations; she was sending a message to someone on the guest list."

Casey's face grew thoughtful. "Doesn't she realize if you dance among the flowers, you risk getting stung by an angry bee?"

Josie snorted softly, "I'll bet she was too busy counting dollar signs to notice the hive on her way to the bank."

I smiled. Trust Josie to cut through the thorns to find the root. If only the truth were as easy to dig up.

"Money is the root of most crimes." Casey pulled the door open, and we walked into the main room. Eunice sat exactly where we left her, eyes fixed on the thinning hordes of media people as they packed their vehicles and left.

She turned, and with a stony stare said, "Now look at what you've done. How will I get word out that the inn is open and ready for business as usual?"

Casey stood beside her. "Eunice, the inn isn't open for business. I promise in a few days you'll be able to address the press."

Josie stood beside Eunice. "And for everything you've gone through, I'll create some advertisements and graphics that you can put on social media and in newspapers to help you."

Eunice tipped her head, the tension in her mouth slowly relaxed into a small smile. "You'd do that for me?

Resting her hand on Eunice's arm, she smiled, "Of course I would. It's what people in Oak Hollow do. Neighbors helping neighbors."

Eunice soaked up Josie's kindness like roses in a drought. Her smile was about saving her business. Too bad she didn't have as much compassion for Adam or the rest of the Posey family. It was doubly sad since Cissy and Rob seemed to have done all they could to help.

Footsteps creaked on the stairs, drawing our attention. Wendy appeared. She wore the same pale green sundress as yesterday. It looked as if she'd slept in it and there was a spot of rusty red on the shoulder strap. Her eyes knit together. "What's going on and where's Andrew?"

Good question. Where was Andrew? But it was the stain that held my attention. Rusty red wasn't a color in her makeup palette, and I only knew one thing that left that particular hue. Blood.

14

───────

"Wendy, why don't you join us?" Casey gestured toward the sofa. "We're waiting for the reporters to leave."

She flashed a questioning glance at Eunice, who said, "I didn't say a word to the reporters before Temperance and Josie arrived. I didn't get the chance."

I swallowed my sharp retort to remind her she had been minutes away from fouling up a murder investigation.

Wendy gave me a wary look. "I'm surprised to see you here."

"Josie and I dropped the trays off to Cissy, and we wanted to check on Eunice to see how she was holding up."

"As you can see, I'm just fine." She crossed her arms over her chest, huffed, sank into the cushions, her eyes narrowing into an accusatory stare.

I never broke my blank expression. "Yes, you are." I nodded to Casey. "Josie and I are going outside. Text if you need us."

She said, "Copy that."

I headed to the main door and then jabbed my thumb toward the kitchen. "Best if we try to slip out unnoticed."

Josie was close on my heels, and we both paused in the kitchen. The quiet sloshing of water being circulated in the dishwasher was the only sound. She asked, "Do you notice anything out of place from yesterday?"

Slowly, I walked around the perimeter of the kitchen. It was tidy, reflecting Eunice's style, except for a few coffee dribbles near the pot and a smattering of crumbs near the cake plate. "Andrew didn't wipe up after he got breakfast for Wendy." I tipped my head, scanning the counters for anything else. "This is the only area where the counters aren't clean. It makes me wonder if the happy couple was already arguing and he was in a hurry."

"I wish he hadn't stormed off." Josie pushed open the back door and walked down the steps.

Satisfied with one final look around, I followed her. The crime scene tape fluttered in the gentle breeze. A pair of birds flew overhead, coasting on air currents.

Josie cleared her throat. "This is shocking, another murder in our quiet town."

"There are people who do bad things everywhere." I squinted my eyes and took in the tent area in front of us. "Josie, what do you see?"

She faced the tent: rows of tables and chairs with linens still in place. All that was missing was the food and dirty dishes to keep scavengers at bay.

"A place where there had been a party?" Her voice rose uncertainly.

"What else?" I wanted her to see what I did. Let her thoughts sift through what was there to what wasn't.

Her gaze swept the space again, moving from right to left and back again. "The potted flowers are missing from the entrances to the tent. On the tables, the centerpieces there were cute potted roses." Her eyes widened. "Casey only gave the approval for the food and dishes to be removed."

I smiled. "Exactly."

In step with each other, we strode down the gentle incline and approached the tent. "Keep your eyes open for the plants."

"Do you think it's a clue?" she asked.

I nodded, pressing my lips into a thin line. "There's no reason for anyone to have moved the potted plants unless there was."

"Huh?" She flashed me a confused look.

"Sorry. Sometimes my brain and mouth don't coordinate the message properly. What I meant to say was, the potted plants have been moved without Casey's say-so. Which means there must be a motive—something to hide. We're going to find those planters and figure out why."

Josie grabbed my arm. "Do you think the killer stashed a clue in one?"

"We're not dealing with someone who had time to think through the details of their crime. They acted out of fear of discovery and moved quickly to cover their tracks while surrounded by party guests. If I had to hide something, I'd hide it in plain sight and everyone would walk past it without a second thought."

"Who had the chance to move the plants?" Josie asked.

I gave her a sidelong look. "Who stayed at the inn last night?"

"Oh." Her mouth formed a large *O.* "Andrew. Wendy. Eunice—but the ladies aren't strong enough to lift the bigger pots. What about Ken?"

"Good question and if there was an accomplice..." I tipped my chin toward the inn. On the upper balcony, Wendy and Ken Grayson stood fixated on us. "Look."

"Dang. Ken could have been the reason Andrew and Wendy argued," she murmured.

I nodded slowly. "We'll ask those questions in a bit. For now, let's give them a little show. Withdrawing my cell, I smiled at Josie. "But first, I'll text Casey to let her know we've got eyes on us."

She chuckled. "Temperance Matthews, are you enjoying the attention from the balcony?"

I smirked. "Enjoying it? Not hardly. The way I see it, it's another piece of the puzzle. It's almost as if they're rehearsing their next act. Should we find something they've hidden?"

Josie rubbed her hands together. "Then let's not disappoint them. We'll find those flower pots, and if I have to empty every single one of them, we'll discover what secrets they tried to bury."

It was my turn to chuckle. "Your determination is admirable. The only hiccup is that we need to find them first."

AFTER CIRCLING the tent and looking under every table, we didn't find a single flower pot or any new clues. I took several deep breaths, forcing away the disappointment. However, there was still considerable ground to cover. I thought about discovering the other camera and T-shirt in the shed. That was hiding in plain sight. I knew in my gut the digital would be the same. We weren't dealing with a calculated killer; the attack was driven by fear and opportunity.

"Where to next?" Josie asked.

I nodded to the shed. "There's no space in there to hide the pots; I'm guessing they'll be behind it."

Grabbing my arm, she stopped me and pointed to the lush flowers in front of the painted lattice. "Look at the flower garden along the width of the porch."

I squinted, "The bed of hydrangeas?" What was she staring at?

"No, behind and between them. Doesn't that look like terra cotta planters?'

I followed her finger as she pointed to the swath of garden. "Good observation." We veered to the right and picked up our pace. My heart quickened. We were finally making progress and not spinning our tires. I could feel it.

As we drew closer, I saw the row of small potted rose bushes that had graced the tables. None of these was big enough to stash a camera. But a memory card could have been slipped into the dirt unnoticed. At this point, I didn't care if it was possibly damaged; there were ways to recover almost anything when it came to digital evidence.

I pulled out my cell and took pictures, counting the number of pots and texting the information to Casey with the statement—*This garden on the west side of the porch needs to be secured. Trust me.*

I didn't wait for or expect an answer. Casey would take care of it. "Do you remember how many large planters were near the tent?"

With hesitation, she nodded. "There were three entrances decorated. At each one, two large pots flanked each support pole. Six."

"And there was one on each end of the buffet table and one near the bar. That's a total of nine." I waited while we each replayed the scene from the previous day in our minds. It was essential to be grounded in the facts before proceeding.

"We're searching for nine." She held up her hand, her index and middle fingers twisted together. "I hope we find them all."

I forced a small smile. "I don't care if we find all of them; we just need the one with the camera."

"You think that we'll find it?" Josie asked as we stood in the doorway of the shed.

"I'm sure of it."

She grinned. "Your sixth sense has kicked in." She stuffed her hands in her pockets; she knew the routine. Hands in pockets helped curb the temptation to touch things we shouldn't. I should have asked Casey for gloves, but if we uncovered a clue, I'd call in an officer and Casey.

Using the hem of my shirt, I clicked the overhead lights on. "Ready?" Then I paused, "Why didn't the lights work yesterday?"

She said, "Maybe someone replaced the bulbs to help with the investigation?"

Which made sense.

"I'll go left and you take the right side?" Josie knew instinctively that most people moved to the right, whether it was to stand in a line, scan a store shelf, or even take a left exit on the highway, which went against how people had trained their brains to process directional information.

I took the right side; it was the most likely place for something to have been stashed. Scanning the interior, it confirmed there was no place to tuck the large planters. It was possible the camera could be in here, but it didn't sit well with me that it would be. Would the killer have used the same hiding location twice? Doubtful. I moved slowly, looking for dust outlines on the workbench, any tools that seemed out of place, or anything else that might indicate someone had been in here after the police had finished searching.

"Josie, did you notice security cameras anywhere?"

"No. Yesterday I asked Eunice when you were in here. I'm sorry I forgot to mention it."

"Don't worry about it. I'm sure Casey confirmed that as well, since we haven't had time to compare notes yet." Why wouldn't Eunice have some sort of camera system? With guests coming and going, and her living at the inn alone, it would have been logical. I'd check with Casey first before discussing it with Eunice, and if, after the investigation was closed, she still resisted, I'd do my best to convince her.

"Did you find anything yet?" Josie asked.

"Not a thing. You?"

"Same."

I wasn't surprised with the lack of clues—I hadn't expected any. "We'll check around back next."

"And if we don't find anything there?"

I quirked a brow in her direction. "Then we search the woods beyond the lawn. The camera is here somewhere. The harder it is to find the large potted plants, the more I'm certain they conceal part of the truth."

We met at the door and divided once again, Josie circling left around the building, and I went right.

"Temperance!"

I dashed around the back of the shed to where Josie was. "What?"

She pointed to a row of four planters; her eyes held a glint of victory. "Five to go."

I took a picture of each planter and then crouched to inspect the base of the flowers and the surrounding dirt to see if it appeared to have been disturbed recently, but they were pristine. "Promising start."

"Is it possible that after moving the first few, the person got tired and decided to stash the rest here?"

"Excellent deduction." I gave her a wide smile. "This could be an important clue."

Her brow furrowed. "How so?"

"Either they were concerned with getting caught, short on time, or not strong enough to move them all." I pressed one foot against a pot, it didn't tip easily. "This has to weigh about thirty pounds." I pressed my finger into the soil. "And it needs watering."

"Why is that important?" she asked.

"If the pots were heavier, it'd be more difficult to move them."

Her eyes lit up. "Unless they used a dolly."

I nodded. "Or another mode of transportation, like a garden cart attached to the lawn mower." I gestured over her shoulder. She followed my arm.

Pulling up the photos I had taken of the crime scene

yesterday, I held them out for her to scroll through. "Look at this. The lawn mower wasn't there."

She gave a low whistle. "Can it be dusted for fingerprints?"

"It sure can." She handed me my phone. I fired off a text to Casey letting her know our recent discovery. "Let's find the last five."

We walked back to where the hose and watering can had been. With it missing, I was sure it had been taken into evidence to get the blood smear analyzed. Most likely, it had come from Adam, but it was best to be sure.

Josie stamped her foot. "Darn it. I was so sure we'd find them sitting right there."

I chuckled. "Don't give up. We'll find them." My gaze was drawn to the longer grass behind the building. It showed signs of being repeatedly tamped down. "We're going that way."

Josie took a step back. "Ew, do you think there are snakes in there?"

I gave her a reassuring smile. "I'll go first. With me clomping through, they'll slither away before you even know they were there."

She shuddered. "Okay. I'll go if you think it's safe."

I walked, taking care as I stepped through the grass. Keeping my eyes on the path in front of me. Not for snakes and other little critters but for clues. The grass was thicker as we walked around the far side of the building until it gave way to a neat, landscaped side yard. A small cedar deck jutted out, and sitting on the lowest step, in a tidy row, were four planters.

My pulse quickened. Under my breath, I said, "One to go."

Josie stamped her foot. "Shoot. We're so close."

"I'm taking a closer look. Can you check out this side of

the building and figure out where we are in relation to the interior?"

"Sure." She ran lightly up the steps and walked the length of the deck, peering in the windows. "It looks like this is a music room. There's an upright piano, a couple of comfy chairs, and a television."

I examined each of the pots, listening to Josie but not responding. The soil was damp but looked untouched. Should I dump them out? I hesitated and shook my head. Not yet. First we needed to find the last planter.

"Temperance," her voice was laced with excitement, "Come quick. I may have found the ninth flower pot."

My heart rate spiked as I dashed across the deck, my sneakers slapping against the wood. Josie stared, unblinking, at a shadowed area. A broken piece of lattice was hanging at a crooked angle from the deck's support posts. Beneath it, half-hidden behind the decorative wood, was a terracotta pot lying on its side. The flowers were strewn across the ground, their roots exposed as dirt was piled up at the sides. It hadn't been carefully placed, but it seemed as if it had been pushed off the deck in an attempt at hiding it underneath the building.

"Do you think the camera's in there?" Josie whispered as if she were afraid someone was lurking nearby.

I wanted to say yes to reassure her we were one step closer to solving the case but I couldn't. My gut told me otherwise. "Not now," I murmured, "but I think that was the original plan, and it didn't work out. Our culprit may have been interrupted."

The air was heavy with silence as Josie and I crept closer, crouching next to me, she asked, "There's nothing?"

When her shadow shifted, the sun washed the ground with light. There was a glint coming from the mound of dirt. I reached out my hand and flicked away a bit of damp soil. My mouth went dry. Victory!

"The camera might not be here," I gave her a side glance, "however, that's a memory card." Those words seemed to energize us both.

"You're kidding!"

I wanted to grab the small plastic device and race to the nearest computer. I rocked back on my heels. "Those are Adam's last words, so to speak. As soon as we can get the device back to the police station, we'll know what happened." Speaking with confidence was one thing, but the feeling deep in my gut told me I was right. The most important clue had been discarded in the dirt, and a secret meant to stay hidden. The realization hit me like a gut punch. My eyes locked with Josie's. "There are two secrets meant to stay hidden: Adam's killer and the secret of the crest. The only question looming… are they connected?"

15

___

*J*osie and I sat on the deck steps while we waited for Casey. When she strode around the corner of the inn and crossed the grass, she gave us a tentative smile. "You found the memory card?"

I pointed to the soil. "Yeah, it looks like we hit pay dirt. A broken terracotta planter with the same flowers as the other eight, and someone tried to shove it under the deck and cover it with the lattice."

Josie let out a nervous laugh. "No pun intended."

"What made you think of looking back here?"

"The lawn mower and lawn cart. It wasn't out yesterday, and the grass leading around the corner had been crushed. I didn't remember seeing it crushed before. The person who moved the planters did it under the cover of darkness. Your team would have found it if they hadn't had to deal with the horde of reporters Eunice was entertaining."

Casey's mouth twitched, although her face remained serious. "That's one way to put it."

"What's Eunice doing now?" I asked.

"She's with Wendy and Ken Grayson, having coffee and cake."

I looked at Josie. "Ken Grayson. We saw him watching us from the second-floor balcony."

She nodded. "Apparently, he stayed here last night as well as Andrew and Wendy."

"Any idea why?"

With a smirk, she said, "If you can believe him, it was to support his cousin in his time of need."

Josie tilted her head. "You don't believe him?"

"I'm sure he was worried about Andrew, but something feels off about the relationship between Wendy and Ken. I can't quite explain it yet, but I will."

I nodded, agreeing with her statement. "We're headed back to my place to dig into the Posey family crest. Do you want me to see what I can find out about Ken and Wendy?"

Josie said, "We can do a social media search."

Casey smiled. "That's good. I'm going to have our team dig into everyone's financials to see if there's a motive for Adam's death. But I'm not making a connection."

"We've speculated that Ken might get a larger cut of the Posey fortune with Adam gone. His mother is Rob's sister, and from one statement Cissy said in passing, money is like vapor through his fingers; he can't hold on to it."

"That's an interesting way to describe your nephew. Even if it is by marriage." Casey snapped a series of pictures before glancing at me. "Did you get everything you need?"

"Yes, thanks." I patted my phone in my back pocket. "We're working on a murder board. Is there anything we should know before we get started?"

"Nothing that I can think of, but what can I tell you?"

Josie nudged my arm. "Security cameras?"

"Right," I said, "Does the inn have any?"

Casey's brow lifted. "That's an interesting question. Eunice doesn't believe in them. When I questioned her, she said it was to protect her guests' privacy."

"What about her protection? If nothing more than against claims of a car hitting another in the parking lot?"

Josie frowned, "It seems foolish when cameras help lower insurance costs."

I snapped my fingers. "That's right. I got a small deduction because I had them at my former bakery. They were instrumental in catching the arsonist and murderer." I hated thinking about those dark days where a man lost his life, and I lost my dream; it still cut to my core. *Correction, your old dream. Version 2.O is going to be just the right mix for now.*

Casey said, "Temperance, maybe it's an avenue you can explore with Eunice. I'm surprised she doesn't have any type of security."

"Me too." I gave a somber nod. "And I plan to do that once the case is solved."

Letting the past cloud my thoughts wasn't going to help Casey close this case. I laced my fingers behind my back and stretched, opening my chest muscles. It was something I often did when I had to force myself to refocus on the task at hand.

"There's nothing else we can do here. But if it's okay with you," I paused and gave Casey a pointed look, "We'll walk through the inn. I'm hoping to overhear something useful. A snippet of conversation, observe body language—the little things that most people dismiss."

She gave a sharp nod. "Stay in touch, and if you uncover anything you think is significant, text immediately. Hopefully tonight I'll get a chance to pop over around dinner time. I was bummed I missed burgers last night."

"Tonight might be pizza. We'll save some." Josie laughed.

As we walked around the building, leaving Casey to wait for the officer to process the scene, Josie asked, "Do you have a plan?"

I glanced at her. "For when we walk through the inn?"

"Yes."

Shaking my head, I frowned. "I'm not going to ask Eunice

about the security cameras right now. But I'm hoping Wendy has heard from Andrew, and maybe Ken will either say something or, through his actions, we can get a read on his intentions with her."

"You think there's something romantic going on between them?"

"Based on what we witnessed two days ago when we delivered the trays, there is. If it's connected to this case, we'll uncover the details."

Josie nodded. "I'll follow your lead and keep my eyes peeled."

I smiled and pulled open the kitchen door, allowing her to go inside first. "You always do."

Angry voices reached us. We rushed through the kitchen into the main room. Eunice was standing behind the check-in desk, her face beet red, lips pressed into a thin line. She narrowed her eyes, "What do you mean you won't pay me for staying here last night?"

Ken's voice boomed, "My cousin was murdered. I wasn't in any condition to drive back to my place, nor were Andrew and Wendy. You should *graciously* comp our rooms. For all we know, you're the reason Adam was killed!"

Eunice's hand flew to her throat, her eyes flashing. "You take that back. If you think you can besmirch this inn's reputation, be prepared for a lawsuit. I won't stand for the likes of you destroying my life's work."

Wendy laid her hand on Ken's arm. "Stop. Rob and Cissy will take care of this. Eunice, roll it into the final bill for the engagement party. They'll pay no attention to the small adjustment."

Eunice's chin lifted as she sniffed. "The invoice was paid ahead of time. I won't send an additional bill to those sweet people while they're grieving the loss of one of their sons; it's just not right. I won't do it."

Ken leaned over the counter, his face inches from hers.

"Then you're going to be out of the cost of two rooms for the night."

Tears welled up in Wendy's eyes. With a catch in her voice, she said, "I asked you to stop." She turned to Eunice. "I'll— I'll pay for both rooms. I just can't deal with this ugliness, especially now that I don't know where Andrew is. He could be lying in the bottom of a ditch the way he tore out of here."

Ken slipped his arm around her waist and held her close to his chest, cupping the back of her head in his hand. This wasn't the way a cousin would hold her. It looked too familiar, too intimate.

"Andrew's just blowing off steam," Ken murmured in a low and soothing tone. I watched as the tension slipped from her shoulders. He continued, "He copes with extreme stress by driving fast, playing classic rock at full volume, and once he's worked things out in his head, he'll be back. You'll see."

Josie nudged my arm to make sure I was taking in every detail unfolding in front of us. Even Eunice, who had been quick with a comment, was silent.

Wendy stepped from his embrace, her cheeks blotched red. She wiped her face with the hem of his shirt and nodded. "You're right. I'm sorry, I shouldn't have lost control."

Holy cannoli! This entire interaction was intimate and careless on their part. Did they honestly think we'd mistake it for family closeness?

Eunice cleared her throat, all business. "Wendy, will you be settling the bill with cash or a credit card? I don't accept checks."

The girl blinked as if she were emerging from a fog. "Um…credit card. It's upstairs in my purse."

Ken quickly offered, "I'll get it for you. Is the door unlocked?"

She nodded. Her fingers tightened on the counter as if it

were the only thing keeping her upright. "Yes." Her voice was soft. "Thank you." This entire scene was surreal.

She glanced out the window with a view of the parking lot. "I wish Andrew would come back." Her gaze locked with mine. "Why are you still here?"

"We were leaving and heard the argument," I said evenly, "We wanted to make sure everything was all right. In case you needed help."

Josie stepped closer to Wendy. "Is there anything we can do before we leave?"

She shook her head; the motion was weary, not the happiest time in her life. "No. Ken will drive me out to the house. I'm sure Andrew is there. It's his haven. That's why he wants to live in that mausoleum." Her lips tipped down.

Wendy exuded the look of a fragile flower beaten down by a rainstorm. The question I had: was she wilting from her grief or putting on an act to hide her thorns?

I gave a curt nod and didn't address either woman specifically. "Then, we'll be going."

Josie crossed the room and gently took Eunice and Wendy's hands. "Temperance and I are just a phone call away if you need anything, anything at all."

Wendy managed a weak smile. "Thank you, Josie, you're very kind."

My eyes were on Eunice. She turned her head, dabbing at her eyes with a tissue. That was the kind-hearted woman I recognized from a few days ago—the kind soul I helped with baked goods.

Softly she said, "Ladies, you've both been so kind. I'm sorry you had to witness my outburst. I'm barely hanging on by a thread, and this has been such a very trying time."

Forcing a small comforting smile when I longed to pepper her with questions, I said, "Eunice, I appreciate your patience with us. We're just trying to help find the truth."

Josie gave their hands one final squeeze before stepping back. "Remember, call us. The offer is sincere."

Wendy placed a hand over her heart, her smile faint. "Thank you."

There was no point in waiting for Ken to come back with Wendy's credit card. I was sure they'd be leaving soon. He didn't seem to like Eunice; however, he was a devoted Wendy fan.

I PUSHED OPEN the back door to my kitchen and whistled. "Hank." It felt as if I had been gone forever instead of a few hours. Josie followed me inside and closed the door, shutting out the problems at least for the moment.

The quick click of toenails against the wood floor brought a smile to my lips even before I saw him. Hank zipped around the hallway corner, his velvet ears flopping and his tail held high as he raced toward me before making a little leap into my arms like we had done thousands of times before, confident I would catch him. He covered my face with puppy kisses as I fell back to my bum, laughing for the first time all day.

Josie grinned and knelt on the floor, scratching behind Hank's ears. "What is it about your little fur baby that sweeps tension from a room like old dust bunnies?"

"I have no idea what his secret is, but I hope he never loses it." I kissed the top of his head and placed him next to me.

I leaned close as if I was confiding in the pup. "Well, Hank. We still have a case. Are you up to helping me and Josie crack it tonight?"

He let out a sharp bark, his tail wagging like a wind-up toy, and a goofy puppy grin, as if to say he was more than ready.

"What's first: setting up the murder board or coffee and sweets?" I asked.

Josie offered me a hand and pulled me to my feet. "I'll make the coffee if you get the board ready. We're super sleuths, we can multitask and do it well."

I laughed, and it felt good. It cleared the noise in my head from everything that had happened over the last three days and released much-needed endorphins.

I withdrew the oversized poster board and easel from the pantry closet. As I extended the legs, I glanced out the kitchen window.

"What on earth is Andrew Posey doing in my driveway, pacing like a caged animal?"

Josie jabbed her finger toward the door. "Ask him to come in, and I'll make a full pot. The research of the crest might be a bit delayed, but he could fill in a few blanks."

I hurried to the door, and Hank hopped onto his bed by the sliding door, his ears standing at attention in case his role as guard dog was needed.

"Andrew?" I called softly. "Come inside." I didn't want to scare him into running away.

He rubbed his hand over his head, his blond hair standing in spikes, his face drawn in a tight grimace. "I didn't know where else to go."

"I'm glad you're here," I said gently, "Josie's brewing a pot of coffee, and we were going to have a snack. Join us?"

16

---

ndrew came inside, glanced around the kitchen, and nodded to Josie. A faint, tired smile graced his mouth when he noticed Hank. "Cute pup."

"Thank you. He's a sweetie." I gestured to a chair. "Have a seat and relax."

As he moved to the chair, I took in the details of his disheveled appearance: his rumpled shirt and jeans, red-rimmed eyes, and untied sneakers. He looked nothing like the man I had seen yesterday—more like a man crushed with grief.

My heart constricted at his suffering. "I'm very sorry about Adam. I only met him once, but I really liked him."

Andrew's fist came down on the wooden table. Hank chirped from his bed and stood as if to ask, *"do you need help?"* I raised a calming hand and pointed to his bed. It was our signal that he could stand down. He did, while his eyes darted from me to Andrew, ready to spring into action for a good ankle chomp if necessary.

"Adam was the best man I knew. He didn't deserve to be murdered, and I demand justice." Even as he spoke the anger-laced words, his shoulders slumped, and fresh tears streaked down his cheeks. Josie ripped off a paper towel and pressed it into his hand.

"We're here to help," she said.

I admired her soothing nature, and she was a good counter to my straightforward questions. But I reined them in for now. There would soon be time to find out what he knew or *thought* he knew.

He dropped his head to the table, his arms dangling at his sides. I looked at Josie. She only shrugged and pulled out a chair next to Andrew. I did the same. We sat on each side of him, letting the silence fill the room.

Sometimes, the best thing to do was wait when someone is in an agitated state like this. Hammering him with questions would either cause him to shut down or give us a distorted view of the events.

Andrew's breath slowed to steady inhales and exhales. He lifted his head and rubbed his eyes. Gaze glued to the table, he said, "I'm sorry."

I placed a hand on his shoulder. "No need to apologize. You've been through a great deal in the last twenty-four hours."

"Yeah." His voice sagged beneath the sadness. "It was supposed to be one of the happiest days of my life, celebrating my upcoming marriage to the woman I love with family and friends. My brother—my best friend—was attacked in a senseless act of violence, ripping him from us." He turned in his chair, the pain in his words shredding my heart. "Who would want to hurt him? He was one of the best people I've known; he was always helping others and standing up for justice. He'd never hurt a fly. I know I keep saying it, but it's the truth."

"Sadly, Andrew," I said, "We won't know the *why* until we get the *who*."

Josie asked gently, "Do you have any ideas?"

I liked that she kept her question to the point without elaborating or leading him in any direction.

He shook his head. "Not a clue. He was out taking pictures. Some people inspired his creative spark, and he asked if he could take some candid photos. He was so excited and said he finally found the direction for a new show." He shook his head, "Can you imagine, a talent like his, developing a new show at our party?" His voice broke as his chin dipped and pulled his shoulders inward. "Now it will never happen."

Uncertain whether the images on the camera could be recovered, I didn't mention the Pad Stone connection or the possibility of holding a posthumous event. That was a conversation for later.

I crossed my legs as I shifted on the chair. "Andrew, I noticed you and Adam wore the same color shirt. Was that intentional?"

He gave a half-hearted smile. "Inside joke. When we were kids, Mom loved dressing us alike. Of course, we hated it and longed for our own identities, but for special occasions like holidays, we always wear something similar. The green shirt was Adam's idea. Mom loves us in green; she says it brings out the colors in our eyes."

It was evident this was a cherished memory and tribute to Cissy.

The coffeepot gurgled, breaking the moment. Josie rose, "I'll get the coffee."

I studied Andrew as he sat expressionless. Getting the conversation back to the party was critical, but he deserved a moment of respite.

Josie quietly moved around my kitchen. Setting the cake platter in front of Andrew, she lifted the dome, adding mugs of steaming coffee for each of us. When she finally sat down again, the faint click of her spoon against the mug broke the heavy silence.

"Temperance?" Andrew lifted the mug and took a slow sip. His voice cracked. "Do you think Adam was killed by mistake, and the attacker thought it was me?"

His question stunned me. Of course, the thought crossed my mind, but since he asked it, there must be a reason that drove him. "It's possible. Would anyone have reason to harm you?"

"Maybe?" The word slipped out as he lowered the mug. Coffee sloshed over the rim as he set it on the table. His hands shook reaching for a napkin.

I thought back to the argument Josie and I had overheard between him and Wendy. The only way I might get the information was to be direct.

"Was this what you and Wendy argued about the night before the party?"

His head snapped up, pausing mid-wipe. "You know about that?"

I held his gaze, letting my silence do the questioning for me.

He slapped his forehead and said, "It's not what you think."

"Then tell me," I leaned forward. "What's the secret and why can't anyone know, especially Ken Grayson, and more importantly, what did your mother do to upset Wendy?"

"The crest." The word sagged more like a curse, or was it relief?

Josie's brows shot to her hairline. I hadn't expected this to be about the crest, but now, I needed to know how it was tied to Adam's death.

Josie asked, "Were you upset because Cissy and Rob wanted the crest to be on the invitations?"

He shook his head. "No. The old crest would have been fine." His jaw flexed. "But Wendy had been digging around the library and discovered a revision that was created after the family settled in Oak Hollow. And stupidly, she used that crest. I guess she wanted to prove to my parents that she was loyal to the family."

"But your father wanted that version suppressed. Do you know why? And what's the Ken connection?"

Andrew picked up his mug, his thumb tracing the rim. For one very long minute, he didn't speak. When he finally lifted his gaze to meet mine, his eyes were haunted by pain and the knowledge that he could hold the key to why his twin was murdered.

"I think," he shifted in his chair "the crest is why Adam was murdered. Someone wants to get their hands on the secret hidden in plain sight for the last hundred years."

Josie sucked in a breath. "Andrew, what's the secret?"

"Do you know Wendy is a commercial realtor? That's how we met—during a negotiation for a large tract of land. I was intrigued by her sharp mind and quick wit. But more than that, she was hungry to succeed in a difficult business. We're alike that way. I want to step out of the Posey shadow and make my mark too."

"Kindred spirits."

He nodded at me. "Yes. For the first time, a woman wasn't interested in my family's money; she comes from money. Together, we could build something separate from our parents."

"Like Adam did?" I asked softly.

"He never had an interest in the family empire."

"Did you resent him for escaping to Austin?"

"Never." He slammed his cup on the table. The word cut through the air, leaving no doubt.

Josie pulled back when I gave her a nod. "Andrew, tell me about the rose and the book."

His mouth gaped open. "You know? Everything?"

I tipped my head from side to side. "Enough. But I'd like to hear it from you."

Praying Josie wouldn't tip our hand, I said gently, "You can trust us."

She placed a comforting hand on his arm. "Andrew, you really can. We want to help the police catch Adam's killer."

His gaze darted from me to Josie and back. "I... I don't know. Maybe I should talk to Wendy first."

"Andrew, this is your family's crest. Wendy passed it to Josie, and she placed it on the invitations, not understanding that the book and the rose held a secret message of some kind. If that's the reason Adam was killed, you need to tell us so that we can track down the truth before anyone else gets hurt."

I let the words hang in the air like comments in a cartoon bubble. Andrew's expression slid from uncertainty to horror. He jumped up and paced the length of the room, wringing his hands and mumbling under his breath. I couldn't catch what he was saying.

"Andrew, talk to us. What's going on in your head right now?"

He whirled around, eyes bright with unshed tears. "Don't you think I haven't put the pieces together? I'm sure this is connected. Don't you think I wished every second of the last nineteen hours that it had been me and not Adam lying in that grass? Don't you think I wished I had never confirmed to Wendy that her suspicions were true?" The tears slipped over his cheeks. "If I could change any of this, I would." He crumpled into a chair.

Josie rushed to his side, and I knelt in front of him. "Andrew," I said, forcing myself to maintain control of my voice even as my emotions seethed inside at the unknown person who had inflicted so much pain on this man, "tell me about the crest." I urged softly. "The secret is about land. It has mineral rights...for silver." His words came out haltingly, each one laced with dread.

I rocked back on my heels. "Silver?" My mind whirled

with silver mining facts. "In this part of the country, it was reported that silver was never in abundance like it was out west."

He shook his head, his eyes fixed on the floor. "There are reports that support its undiscovered wealth. Somehow, the Posey family acquired it shortly after arriving in the United States."

I rose and paced the length of the room. Hank lifted his head, watching me as I turned. "During the argument you had with Wendy, she said *he* was asking questions, and it would be harder now that Cissy wanted the crest on the invites. Who is he?"

"Ken."

My gut tightened. "Your cousin? How did he learn about it? I would think, given his reputation among the family, the supposed silver would be like a dog with a meaty bone."

"Yeah," he gave a grim nod, "It'd be irresistible to him. He'd figure out a way to stake a claim to the land, get investors to sink money into mining the land, but there's another catch."

Josie said, "You mean in addition to not knowing where the land actually is located?"

At last, Andrew looked at us. "I know where the parcel is. It's pristine, left to its wild state. There are brooks running through the property, wildlife is abundant, and endangered reptiles and other animals live there. I even discovered three bald eagle nests at the top of the white pines that are close to one of the larger streams."

Josie's breath caught. "You've walked the land?"

He nodded. "Wendy and I did. I never should have taken her there and stuck to the family's rule of it never being acknowledged as true."

"Why?" I asked, leaning against the counter. "Is there more to the story?"

"My parents decided to keep the secret so that the land

wouldn't become a place for treasure hunters. Right now, people assume the town owns the overgrown land. I wanted our family to turn it into a conservation area with day-hiking trails, so the average person could enjoy the beauty, but Dad ignored me. I figured that someday, when I inherited the estate, it's what I'd do."

"Wendy disagrees?" Josie asked.

"That's putting it mildly. Remember, she's out to make her mark and her own fortune. She saw this as the best and quickest way to do it."

Tapping my chin with my index finger, I said, "Your family would never agree; it's rooted in the Posey family legacy." My thoughts raced. *How is this tied to Adam?*

"And Ken knows because Wendy told him." It wasn't a question, and with Andrew's silence, it confirmed my suspicions. "What was your plan?"

He tipped his head. "I didn't have one. Well, at least until Adam came home. I told him what Wendy did. Of course, he was furious, but said that after the party we'd sit Wendy and Ken down and make it crystal clear the land would never be rezoned, that we'd fight it together."

"And now you won't have the chance." I leveled my gaze at Andrew. "What else aren't you telling me?"

"About the land? Nothing, I swear."

His words trembled, betraying the worry he felt. He was holding something back, and it could be a game-changer; I just had to push harder.

"Andrew. What's between Wendy and Ken?"

His eyes widened. "Oh no. You figured that out, too?"

I cocked a brow, folding my arms over my midsection to let him know that I'd wait for him to finish his statement.

After a few moments, I prompted him, "Ken's a gambler and not in the casual way, right?"

Andrew nodded.

"Did he get in over his head, and that's why he concocted this scheme?"

Another nod, heavier this time.

"Why did Wendy betray your confidence and tell him?"

Andrew's jaw flexed. "He went to her for money to pay off his debts. Flirted with her and told her I had bailed him out before, but he didn't want to bother me. I *think* it might have turned into something more, but I'm not sure. What I do know, he used whatever happened between them to black-mail her. Ken convinced her to pressure my dad into signing over the land to him. I still don't know how he thought it would work, but they were scheming."

Josie jumped to her feet, daggers shot from her eyes. "Ken thought that if he controlled the land, Wendy would help him move forward with destroying an ecosystem filled with endangered wildlife?"

Andrew gave a defeated nod. "I know, it sounds ludi-crous. But yes, and here we are."

I pulled a chair over and sat down at his eye level, letting the silence grow to sharpen his thoughts. "Andrew, look at me and answer these next questions. But think very carefully before you do." I waited until I had his eyes locked on mine. Without softening the questions as they formed, I said, "After all this, do you still want to marry Wendy? Even though you believe she and Ken are responsible for killing your brother?"

17

———

*A*ndrew flinched. To his credit, he never broke eye contact. "She's not capable, but Ken is. Family means nothing to him except a bank account. I know what's really going on between them. I've watched them when they think no one is looking—the intensity, the connection. If she's in love with him, the wedding is off."

"Are you going to confront her?" I maintained my gaze.

He straightened. "I'm going to be direct. Trying to drop subtle hints and funny comments hasn't worked. But before that happens, I needed to know; why attack Adam? To keep him from helping me protect Rose Hill? They won't get away with it."

The man didn't flinch; the earlier tremor, gone. He was sincere. I walked back to the table, picked up my coffee mug, and sipped the now-cold bean water. I grimaced.

Josie slipped the mug from my hand and popped open the microwave. "Sixty seconds will fix that look."

When it beeped, Hank looked up and gave an approving woof.

I took the mug and let the heat seep into my cells, like water in a desert.

"If you're sincere, and I believe you are, Josie and I have questions. Are you prepared to answer them honestly? And in full disclosure, we spent a couple of hours with your parents this morning and promised them we'd do our best in helping the police find the guilty party."

He tipped his chin toward the microwave. "Mind if I reheat my coffee? Then you can ask as many questions as you want. I have all the time in the world." He forced a smile that didn't reach his eyes. "Or until the coffee pot runs dry."

An hour later, my murder board was filled with scribbled words, lines connecting ideas, and at its center were two names in a circle—Wendy and Ken.

I dropped into the kitchen chair. "Andrew, we need you to go back to the inn and talk to Wendy privately about her relationship with Ken. Until we have that piece of the puzzle, we won't know if it was Ken working alone or if they attacked Adam together." I glanced at Josie before saying, "I noticed a rusty red color on her sundress. It looks like dried blood. Any idea how that got there?"

He nodded. "I was hugging Wendy when my nose started to bleed."

I tipped my head. "When was that?"

"After the panic attack. It's a stress response. The doc said it was fairly common and nothing to worry about as long as it stopped quickly. Of course, she was furious and said I ruined her dress."

He turned to Josie. "If you were a girl like Wendy, driven and marrying the man you said you loved, would you ever get mixed up with a low-life cousin? Help him to swindle your future family out of a protected piece of land? All for a quick buck?" Clearly, the sundress was forgotten.

"Andrew, that's not a fair question." Josie placed a steady hand over his. "That goes against everything I am at my core.

The moment I said yes to your proposal, my loyalty would be to you and your family. I'd stand with your father to protect that land from unscrupulous people like Ken."

"I picked the wrong girl." He swallowed hard. "Ken was smart and played Wendy's ambition. With her connections and knowledge of how to work the permit process, find developers who'd turn a blind eye, and investors who love large returns…they could make a killing."

"Andrew," I had to choose my next words carefully. "We need your help to separate Ken and Wendy; to uncover the truth. From a distance, they look strong like a mighty oak, until lightning strikes, revealing its rotten core."

"Am I the lightning bolt in the scenario?" He looked between Josie and me.

I nodded. "We'll help you come up with questions to ask her, and we'll be close by."

"You won't be alone," Josie said. "We'll be at the inn in another room where we can hear everything."

Hank gave a low, deep woof.

"Sounds like Hank thinks it's the right call." I gave Andrew a reassuring smile. "Our security detail is in full agreement. Are you?"

He looked at the murder board as though he was seeing it for the first time. I was glad the crime scene photos were still on my cell. That would have been brutal for him to have those visuals living in his head for the rest of his life. The horror of his brother's murder was enough to deal with.

"I need to talk with my parents first. They should know about my suspicions and what we're going to do." He stood. "You won't change your mind about helping me?"

"Not a chance we're backing out. I'll fill in Officer Butler and Sergeant Franklin. It's best to keep them abreast of this new information so they can make the arrest."

His shoulders sagged as if the weight of the truth might be more than he could carry.

"One good thing might come out of Adam's death," he said softly. "Maybe I can convince Dad to donate the land to the state's nature conservancy and have it officially protected from gold diggers." A wry smile tugged at his lips. "Or in this case, silver diggers."

I patted his shoulder. "It's good to see you can find a silver lining."

His smile was a little wider this time. "Don't think I'm being disrespectful to Adam. Talking with you and Josie has given me something to do, to get justice for my brother."

"In the meantime, should we come up with some questions to ask Wendy?" Josie asked.

He nodded. "That would be helpful, and maybe a few for Ken so I can pin him to the wall. Ones that would be impossible for him to evade."

"We can do that," I reassured him. "When do you want to meet at the inn?"

He said, "I'll call Wendy and ask her to stay there so we have some time alone without the family hovering. Judging by the parking lot this morning, the guests have checked out. Once the reporters are gone, we should be able to talk freely."

"The reporters are gone," I said. "Officer Butler made them leave, and Eunice has been instructed not to speak to the press."

"That sweet woman couldn't hurt a fly." He said, "She was so kind to us last night, even fixing a light supper despite the fact we weren't hungry."

"Andrew, does anyone else have access to the library at home, outside the family?" I asked.

"Mom lets Eunice borrow books, and of course, the extended family—like my aunt and uncle—do too. Why?"

"I'm wondering if anyone, not on our suspect list, could have come across the crest information."

Josie said, "Like a window washing company, perhaps?"

He shook his head. "That's a stretch. We've used the same

companies for years to do the deep cleaning, and our regular staff are like family. We don't treat anyone like hired help. It's not like previous generations, which might have."

I gave a thoughtful nod. Not everyone was as they seemed. "What time should we meet you at the inn?"

He turned his wrist over to examine the face of his watch. That was unusual; it's common for military personnel to wear a watch this way to protect the face from scratches. Andrew's wasn't a rugged field watch. It was a sleek, high-tech smart watch. I glanced at Josie, and my eyes landed on the watch, where her brows were furrowed together as she studied him.

"Were you in the military?" she asked.

He glanced up, surprise etched over his face. "Me? No…" then his mouth curved into a smile. "The watch? Texts pop up on the screen. If I'm with people who shouldn't see the messages, it's easier to wear it like this. It took some getting used to, but now it's natural."

I wondered if that included Wendy, but I kept that question to myself. Despite the doubts he had about their relationship, they were still engaged to be married.

He asked, "Can you give me three hours? Which'll give me time to talk with my parents and get a bite to eat, since, other than the coffee and cake, I haven't eaten food that doesn't contain copious amounts of sugar. It's going to take all my strength to deal with Wendy. I need to be sharp." A frown settled on his face. "Should I have Ken there, too? Maybe I can get them to confess to everything at the same time."

"No." The word cracked out like a command.

His head snapped toward me. "Temperance, why not?"

"In my experience, co-conspirators never break when they're questioned together. It's best to keep them separate so neither knows what the other has said. Then the truth usually surfaces."

Throwing up his hands, he slapped his thighs, magnifying

his frustration. "This whole idea—me trying to trap Wendy into telling me a truth I don't even know exists—is calculated. I love her. The last thing I want to believe is that she's guilty of attempting to swindle land from my family. I can't even begin to grasp the possibility she was involved in my brother's death, or…" his voice broke as he pressed her hands over his face "that she might have wanted me dead."

I stepped closer to him; my word choice was deliberate. "Is it easier to accept your cousin might have intended for you to be the victim?"

His jaw flexed. "Of course not. Once he started down the road of a professional gambler, although he's got a poor record of winning, his jealousy surfaced. We had a huge argument. I got tired of him always begging for money for one loan shark or another. The last time I helped him was about six months ago, and I told him, 'The Ken's Handout account' was empty." He grasped the edge of the table to steady himself.

"After that," I pushed him a little hard but kept my tone soft. "Did he keep coming back to you?"

He shook his head and sat in the chair Josie had pushed over for him. "No. He didn't get the dangers of owing the wrong sort of person. Like I said before, I knew he went to Wendy and she gave him money. And then, a few weeks ago, I was taking the shortcut through the park downtown on my way to the post office to get those fancy wedding stamps Wendy wanted. You know the kind with the doves and hearts?"

I nodded. "I do."

He continued, "Wendy was on a bench. I thought she was taking a break between clients. I called out to her, but I guess she didn't hear me. I changed direction, heading over to her when I noticed Ken running toward her. She stood, and they embraced. Not a kiss but a very tight hug. I froze, turned, and hurried in the opposite direction, pretending I hadn't seen a thing. That night, over dinner, I casually brought up what she had done during the day, mentioning any new clients or properties, all part of our normal conversation. She never mentioned the park. Or seeing Ken."

"Ouch," Josie muttered softly. "That must have been a gut punch."

"You have no idea." He shook his head. "Ever since I got here, this has been the worst roller coaster ride of my life. My stomach's twisted in knots, my mouth's dry, and my heart's pounding so hard I think it's going to burst from my chest. I wish I'd never stopped here. I should have gone back to the inn and picked up Wendy and gone home to help my parents plan Adam's funeral."

I dropped to one knee beside him. "Look at me." Hopefully, the urgency in my voice would give him an emotion to focus on other than the emotional and physical chaos at war in his body.

"Temperance, I can't do this." His words were faint as hope died in his eyes.

"Andrew, if the roles were reversed, would Adam give up on helping me?" I softened my tone. "And I'm sorry if my question sounded harsh, but Josie and I need you. Your parents have asked for it, and in many ways, Adam's asking too."

He took three slow, deep breaths. With each inhale, his spine straightened a little more. He stood tall with his shoulders back. "You're right. This is one of the last things I can do for him. Thank you for being blunt. I'll meet you at the inn later, and you'll text me a few questions to get me started talking with Wendy?"

"Yes." I glanced at Josie and she gave a quick nod. "We'll send a few for Ken too, just in case we get lucky and he's still there."

With a sharp, disgusted snort, he muttered, "Are you kidding? I realize now he's going to stick to Wendy like gum on your shoe. He won't take the chance of letting her out of his sight if he can help it. Especially with the land deal up in the air."

I brushed off my knees and gave him a brief half-hug. "Andrew, what you're facing over the next few hours is tough stuff. The only request I have is that you don't tell anyone you've been here, not even your parents. We need the element of surprise, and as soon as you tell your parents, they're going to want action."

"Temperance," Josie said carefully, "we want Rob and Cissy to know what we're doing.

I drew in a slow breath. "Right." My thoughts raced to how we could control the events that would spiral after Andrew spoke to them. "Rob and Cissy have lost their son, and Andrew may still be in danger. They're going to want to act."

Turning to him, I kept my voice steady. "Andrew, tell them, but remind them we need time to speak with Pad Stone about the photos."

"Photos?" he asked.

"We have one camera Adam was using yesterday, and the memory card from the digital and the black and white film. It had been hidden, so I'm hopeful Adam took a picture of a critical piece of evidence."

"Could that indicate he was the intended victim?" Andrew asked, his eyes narrowing, "Someone killed Adam because he took pictures?"

"If he were the intended target, there could be evidence in his pictures, or it's possible he wasn't. We just don't know yet." I kept my voice firm. "But I promise you, we *will* find out who did this."

His voice dropped to a whisper, his words unyielding. "Whoever is responsible has no idea what's coming their way."

18

––––––

*E*n route to the police station, my cell rang. Josie glanced at the screen. It's Rob Posey."

I answered. "Hello."

"Temperance, I wanted you to know Pad Stone has arrived at the station. He's meeting with Officer Butler and Sergeant Franklin. He's hoping to see you and Josie soon. I told him how you're helping us."

"Thank you. Casey called and said Mr. Stone had already reviewed the memory card. He had a few things to discuss with her, but Josie and I were anxious to learn what it was, along with the status of the film."

I heard a grim chuckle.

"I shouldn't have underestimated your involvement." He cleared his throat. "Thank you for encouraging Andrew to come home. As devastating as this has been, I'm going to do everything I can to protect him. If someone mistook Adam for his brother, they chose the wrong family to target. Which includes taking my land."

The razor-sharpness of his words sent a chill racing down my spine. "Rob, we need to stay within the guidelines of the law. Don't go looking for revenge."

Silence filled the line. I glanced at Josie, whose worried expression matched how I felt.

Finally, he said, "I don't need to. I have you, Josie, Pad Stone, and the entire police force on our side. Whoever did this won't slip through the cracks of the system."

"Your confidence is reassuring. Will Andrew stay at the house until I call to let you know we're ready to meet him at the inn?"

"He's agreed to stay, but Cissy had to convince him it was the right decision. Between us, he doesn't want to leave Wendy alone with Ken for that long. Whatever's going on between those two, well, the damage's been done. I expect the engagement will be called off once I confront those two about their plans for Rose Hill and the guilty party is arrested for killing Adam."

Josie's eyes widened, shock written on her face. Rob confirmed Rose Hill was real and had known the entire time. Too bad he hadn't been transparent with us from the start.

"Why pretend you were unaware of the authenticity of Rose Hill?" I asked.

Josie nodded in agreement and jabbed a finger at the phone, almost like she was jabbing Rob. I couldn't help but smile.

"I'm sorry. I've spent years denying it exists. It was the only way I knew to protect the land. According to family records, once the silver was discovered and the decision was made to never mine it, denial became our strategy. Private land conservation gained traction in the mid-to-late twentieth century. In hindsight, I should have drafted a formal documentation plan to protect the land after inheriting it. Until recently, there had been no issue using the denial method."

Josie tipped her head back and closed her eyes before asking, "You didn't think it was a matter of time before the truth surfaced?"

I parked in front of the police station and turned off the car. This conversation was important: too important to rush.

In a weary voice, he said, "Not really. I mean that might sound naïve, but when I married Cissy and confided in her about Rose Hill, she agreed to keep things as they were. When the boys reached an age where they understood the gravity of the situation, they agreed too. We never brought Wendy into that family secret; she wasn't a Posey yet. Or Ken either. As my nephew, he wouldn't be in any position to inherit any part of my estate."

I asked, "What about Wendy? Would you have told her after the wedding?"

"Yes."

"Rob, we understand how difficult this time is for you, Cissy, and Andrew." I hesitated to include Wendy. Since yesterday, when we had seen her—and she wasn't grief-stricken over the situation—Adam's death seemed like an inconvenience to her. "I'm sure once Andrew talks with Wendy, she'll be able to clear up…"

"Ha." Rob snorted. "She thinks she's smarter than the rest of us. I've made some calls to my contacts in the industry to get the word out—Rose Hill is off limits. It will never be sold."

Josie frowned. "Do you think that's necessary?"

"The donation process will take, at a minimum, three months," Rob said firmly. "I want to make sure anyone who's interested knows it's not going to happen."

"I agree, that's a smart move." I nodded toward the building. "We're at the station now. I'll be in touch later."

"All right. You ladies stay safe." He disconnected.

Josie's eyebrow twitched. It was something that had just started to happen when she was nervous. Staring at the building, she said, "The police station is one of the safest places in town… Well, except the bank vault. Right?"

"Rob was speaking off the cuff. We're not in danger unless we drink the coffee." I winked and pushed open the door. "Ready?"

"Sure." Josie got out, and I locked the car.

She said, "I'm curious to meet Padraic Stone."

"Other than him being a cop and a photographer, do you know anything more?"

"He lives in Loudon with his wife, Ellie, which is a short half-hour flight from here. She owns a gallery: The Looking Glass. They met when she had been attacked and he was exhibiting some of his work there."

We climbed the steps. My hand hovered near the door handle. "How do you know all that?"

She grinned and lifted a shoulder in a casual shrug. "It's in his bio, on his website—well, most of it. The rest I found by doing a deeper search."

"When did you have time to research Pad Stone?"

Laughing, she said, "When you took Hank out before we left. Someone needed to be prepared. You're not the only one who knows her way around a keyboard and search engine."

I pulled open the heavy glass and metal door. We entered the small, sterile lobby. Ahead of us was a wall, with a solid metal door to the right of the bullet-resistant window. A police officer I didn't recognize was on the other side. Approaching the window, I said, "Temperance Matthews and Josie Shaw to see Officer Butler."

He nodded. "Have a seat and I'll let her know you've arrived."

We did as he instructed and sat with our feet flat on the floor in two uncomfortable, wooden, straight-back chairs. The beige linoleum floor showed two sets of footprints leading from door to door. Someone crossed the surface while it was still wet. On the wall was a mission statement in bold letters. Under that was a bulletin board with a missing persons and pet area, community events to attend, bicycle safety week, neighborhood watch groups, and how to file a complaint. All pretty standard stuff.

Josie spoke softly, "What do you think was on the memory card?"

"Pictures of guests, the catering staff, and I'm not sure what else catches a photographer's attention. Flowers maybe?" I glanced at the digital clock on the wall. Each minute dragged. I was eager to enter the inner sanctum.

Josie said, "We know his muse was in overdrive since he specifically asked people if he could take their pictures for a potential show."

I nodded, "True." The word came out slowly.

The door opened. Casey held it with her hip. "Ladies. Come in." She gestured to the desk. "Sign in and grab visitor badges. You're gonna be here a while."

I pinned a plastic badge holder to my shirt, and when Josie was done, we followed Casey down a hallway, passing two small rooms, the officer's break room, and another one where the Sarge sat behind a desk. He nodded before Casey ushered us into a conference room.

A tall, broad-shouldered man sat at the table, drumming his fingertips in a steady rhythm on the metal surface. Black jeans, well-worn cowboy boots, and a black T-shirt gave him a dangerous look. His chestnut brown hair, cut short, was more police officer-like. When he turned, his amber eyes locked on mine, as if they could uncover all a person's secrets. For the first time in two years, I assessed him with the same precision. He was no ordinary photographer and cop. I tipped my head. Could he have been with one of the agencies?

Casey said, "Padraic Stone, this is Temperance Matthews and Josie Shaw. Consultants for the Oak Hollow PD."

He shook our hands; his grip was firm. "Casey's filled me in on your expertise. Good to be working with you—unofficially, of course."

I narrowed my eyes. "And your background?"

A low chuckle filled the room, friendly like, causing the tension to ease from between my shoulder blades. Did he guess what I was thinking?

"I'm a friend of the victim's father and a professional photographer. I'm here in that capacity. Nothing more."

Josie looked from Pad to me. "What's going on?"

I shook my head. "Nothing."

He gestured for us to sit. "I've got the digital images ready for review. I've scanned them and I don't see anything unusual. However, since I wasn't at the event, I'm at a disadvantage. Casey thought you might have insight."

She handed us pads and pencils, put bottles of water on the table, and dimmed the lights. "Note anything you feel we should discuss. The image number will appear in the lower left."

At a slow but steady pace, we reviewed each photo. Adam captured the essence of the day's happiness. The photos weren't a random assortment, like I would have done. Candid shots and posed images of family groups rolled across the screen.

When a series of floral images began, I leaned forward. "Pad, can you slow down? All the pots were moved overnight, and I'd like to confirm the locations."

His eyes narrowed. "You're trying to figure out who could have moved them?"

Josie nodded, "There were nine pots on the ground and they were at least thirty pounds. The table arrangements were moved to a flower bed near the inn. But the rest we think were relocated using a lawn tractor and cart."

He glanced at Casey. "Did any guests report hearing the tractor during the night?"

"We're working the phones now," Casey said, "contacting everyone who checked out prior to Temperance and Josie making the discovery."

I frowned. "I'm assuming you asked Wendy, Ken, and Eunice?" I dropped my chin to my chest as it hit me—I never asked Andrew.

"They said they didn't hear a thing. The central air conditioner's on the fritz, so Eunice had window units running in their bedrooms."

Josie murmured. "How convenient."

Pad tapped the table. "Anyone could have moved those containers with a folding dolly and the cart. It would take a few hours, but it's possible it was a one-man job.

Again, Josie murmured, "Or woman."

Her gaze circled the table as we stared at her. "What? I think it was Wendy. She had a motive: money. She has admitted that the family hasn't warmed up to her. Maybe she meant to kill Andrew for an insurance payout." Josie snapped her fingers, "Or, what if, she thought the best time to get Rob to sign over Rose Hill and the mining rights was while he was consumed with grief?"

Pad said, "You know about Rose Hill?"

I gave him a side eye. "You do too?"

He nodded. "Rob kept nothing from me when we talked after I arrived."

Casey gave a thoughtful nod. "Wendy could have been that devious. But regarding any insurance money, they're not married yet. She has no spousal claim to it."

"Unless Andrew had changed the beneficiary for his estate." I said quietly. "After all, the wedding's in eight weeks and he's a planner."

Pad focused on me. "How do you know that?"

"When he was at my place earlier, he decided he would confront Wendy about everything. Including his suspicions that something is going on between her and Ken."

He and Casey exchanged a look—one that meant there was no way they wanted a confrontation between their prime suspects and the victim's brother.

"That comes after he tells his parents what he suspects and already knows Wendy has done for Ken regarding Rose Hill. That's why Andrew's practicing the questions we drafted for him. When he sits down with them separately, he'll be ready. Of course, Josie and I promised we'd be close by, along with Casey, for protection. And with a bit of luck, an arrest."

He nodded, and appreciation warmed his eyes. "What else do you know?"

I gave him a small smile. "Have I captured your attention?"

"Completely." His respectful gaze never wavered." Tipping his head, he said, "Go on."

"Ken has a bad habit of owing the wrong kind of people money."

Josie chimed in, "A lot of money."

I exhaled. "Until six months ago, Andrew was Ken's personal banker. Since then, the funds dried up when Andrew cut him off. He's certain Ken borrowed money from Wendy. I use that term very loosely since he'll never repay it. After they discovered the secret of Rose Hill and the silver mine underneath it, it's not a stretch to guess Ken thought it was a solution to his financial problems, and as a bonus, it was a sweet real estate deal for Wendy."

Casey said, "Also, he probably thinks he's entitled to it since his mother is Rob's sister."

Pad shifted in his chair. "Was she disinherited?"

"I looked into that last night, and her bank account is more than healthy. And Ken? He received a substantial sum of money upon the death of Grandfather Posey. But he's squandered every penny gambling. I think the man *is* out of options and has gotten desperate," I said.

"You think he killed his cousin?" Pad's voice was quiet but carried the weight of granite.

Casey pushed back her chair, and the legs scraped the

floor. "Someone in that inn killed him. I feel it in my gut." She stood at the back of the room. "We need to finish with these pictures. If I were Andrew, I'd be anxious to get these conversations over with."

"And I have film to develop." Pad tapped the keyboard and the image changed on the screen.

Casey flipped the lights on after we reached the end. I balled my hands in my lap. "All those pictures and not one holds a clue."

Josie nodded. "Their beautiful party pictures. The one thing I noticed is that Adam was only in a couple of the group photos. Any idea who took those?"

I sucked in my lower lip. "Who would he trust with his camera?"

Josie turned her chair from the screen. "I'll bet he handed it off to someone close by, maybe a wait staff member or another guest."

Pad shook his head. "Not likely. His camera isn't a low-end consumer version. He'd only hand it off to someone he trusts."

Puzzled, I glanced at Josie. "Besides his family, who would Adam trust with his equipment? Were any of his friends there?"

"Not that I'm aware of. It was more about Andrew and Wendy. Just because the boys were twins doesn't mean they have the same friends."

"Maybe his aunt, Ken's mother?" I mused. "Max Griffin? He's a professional event planner and could be familiar with camera equipment."

Josie turned back to the screen. "Scroll back a few shots before Adam's in the pictures."

Pad did as she requested.

"Stop." She pointed at the screen, a small smile tugged at the corner of her lips. "There. Eunice is just at the edge of the frame. As a friend of the family, she'd be the perfect person to snap some keepsake photos."

I slapped Josie a high five. "Well done." Then my thoughts turned dark. If Eunice had the camera, she may have witnessed more than she knew. Could she be in danger too?

I shot to my feet. "We have to get to the inn. Now."

19

We followed close behind Casey's police car as we raced toward the inn. Josie dialed Andrew on speaker phone. When he answered, I said, "Hi Andrew." Did that sound casual enough?

"Temperance, is it time?"

I looked at Josie; she nodded.

"Yes, we're on our way to the inn. How are your questions? Ready to talk to Wendy?"

"Yes, Mom and Dad insist on coming, but I said I'd clear it with you first."

I bobbed my head from side to side. On one hand, they were directly involved, but on the other, the fewer people there were, the better in case this went sideways.

"Temperance?"

"I'm still here. Just thinking. Can you ask them to stay home for now? The police know the plan, and they'll be there to support you, from a distance, so you can get the truth."

Josie crossed fingers and forearms too. I smiled at the slight comic relief.

"We can call them when we have answers."

He exhaled. "I'll do my best, but you know my parents—they're not easily dissuaded."

"I have faith you can convince them. We'll see you there in what, fifteen minutes?"

"Give or take a couple of minutes. Bye." The line went dead.

My hands tightened on the steering wheel. "That went better than I thought."

"Don't be surprised if Cissy and Rob show up. Maybe not with Andrew, but if my son were about to confront his brother's potential killer, I wouldn't be sitting home waiting for an update."

"Oh, you're right. I never thought of it like that."

I slowed, clicked on the blinker, and turned onto the road that led us out of town. "I hope Eunice is okay."

Josie's voice softened. "She's one tough lady. When her husband died, I thought she'd sell the inn, but she kept it going despite the challenges."

We drove in silence for several minutes before she asked, "Who do you think it is? Ken or Wendy or both?"

"As much as I'd like to say they're in this mess together, my gut's telling me this was a solo act. Wendy's caught up in some nonsense about the land, and she's guilty of making poor decisions, but I don't think she's the killer."

"So…you think Ken killed his cousin?"

"Adam saw something. He realized what Wendy and Ken wanted to do with Rose Hill, and he would stop them. They argued, tempers flared. Ken grabbed the brick and struck him. When Ken realized what he'd done, he hid Adam's camera in the shed and cleaned up as best as he could with the shirt and hose."

Her brow furrowed. "Do you believe what Andrew said about the blood on Wendy's dress?"

"Yes. For Wendy to have hit Adam, she's not tall enough.

Adam was over six feet; his attacker had to be taller and stronger than Wendy."

"Like Ken."

I nodded. "Yes." Slowing, I followed Casey down the gravel driveway. The inn came into view with flowers in full bloom. It looked like a scene from a Hallmark card.

Eunice waved to us from the porch, —almost as if she expected us.

Casey, Josie, and I walked up the tidy front walk.

"Afternoon, ladies. Who are you here to see?" Her smile faltered for a half a heartbeat, or maybe it was my imagination.

The stress of this case and the emotional weight were taking a toll on me.

"Andrew's coming out to talk with Wendy and Ken." I looked over my shoulder to double-check their cars were still in the lot.

"They just went in to grab some freshly-baked oatmeal cookies. Would you like some?" She rose from the chair. "I'll make tea, too."

"Not right now." I pointed to the seat she had vacated. "It would be best if you stayed out here while they talk."

"Ken, Wendy, and Andrew are going to chat?" She turned the rocking chair to face the door and windows. "Well, I need a ringside seat. Voices travel around here, you know."

I noticed the windows were open and there were no air conditioners on the first floor. "Did someone come out to fix the AC?"

"Not until tomorrow. I wasn't going to pay double time for a Sunday visit. Besides, I expect it will just be me here tonight. I don't mind if it gets a little warm upstairs. It reminds me of when Fred and I first moved in here. Back then, there wasn't any air conditioning at all, and we managed to get by. Of course, we didn't have many guests, but once we made the improvements and installed central air, nothing could stop us." A shadow flickered across her face. "Until he died."

"I'm sorry you've had a rough go of things since he passed away."

Eunice's lips thinned, her eyes hard. "Rough? It would have been easier if he'd taken out life insurance. I had begged him. He only bought a policy on *my* life. I told him women outlived their men. He lied straight to my face—said he took care of it. After the funeral, I tore this place apart looking for insurance paperwork, and even talked to our agent. Nothing—not one penny to help me keep this place going." She thrust her chin up. "If he had cared like he said, he'd have made sure I was provided for. But he didn't."

I looked to Josie, silently pleading for help.

"Eunice, you've done great things with the inn. Hosting events and running winter specials…it's all helped."

The older woman's expression softened as she smiled at Josie. "It was your beautiful advertisements and the work you did on the website, that's what really drew people in."

Josie said, "You're sweet. I was happy to help, and we'll keep the campaigns going once the police finish their investigation, ensuring everyone knows how special Oak Hollow Hideaway Inn still is. You'll be booked every weekend."

A flicker of excitement didn't completely fade as it flashed over her face. "Good. Sadly, with Adam Posey dying on my property, it might attract more than just guests. Curiosity seekers, reporters…maybe even a documentary crew. You know, he's a big deal in the art world. There are people who'd want to walk in his last footsteps, and for the price of a room at the inn, they'd get the chance."

She lifted her shoulder in a casual shrug, but something lingered in her eyes that chilled me to the bone.

The crunch of tires on gravel drew my attention, and I was happy for the distraction.

Eunice wasn't coming off as the nice lady I originally thought.

Andrew's SUV, the one that had almost run us off the road earlier, parked next to mine.

I lifted my hand in greeting while Josie continued to talk to Eunice, reaffirming the importance of the police and me handling the situation. "After all, Eunice, it's in your best interest."

Since her comments about the potential for increased business, I didn't want to be around her right now. Stressful situations didn't always bring out the best in people...and in her case, I hadn't liked how she handled stress.

Crossing the porch, I hurried over to Andrew. He stared at the inn, not moving.

"Hey. You got here fast." It was a light and easy comment. One that would get him to look at me. Dang, his gaze slid past me to the left of the building and locked on the crime scene tape. He flinched and rounded his shoulders inward at the visible reminder.

I touched his arm. "You don't have to do this. Casey can question them at the station."

His gaze focused on me. His eyes were shining with tears that he refused to let fall.

"I've got to do this. For Adam." He took one faltering step forward. Then another. And another.

Each step seemed like he was walking through heavy, wet sand, moving forward as if sheer will was propelling him.

"Andrew!" Wendy ran down the porch steps and flung her arms around his neck. "Where have you been? I know you told me not to worry, but I did." She brushed a feather-light kiss over his mouth. "Come inside. Ken and I just set up coffee and cookies in the main room. If you want, we can have it on the porch or even under the maple trees. Whatever you'd like..." Her voice trailed off when she realized Andrew wasn't responding to her chatter or hug.

"Wendy." His voice sliced through the warm air like a stiff Arctic wind.

Her arms dropped to her sides. She took a halting step back. "What's wrong?"

"We have to talk, and then I need to speak with Ken."

"Over coffee and cookies?"

"This isn't a pleasant conversation." Andrew's voice was flat. "We'll do it one-on-one." He nodded to me. "Temperance will be in the room."

She licked her lips as the color drained from Wendy's face. "What are you accusing me of?"

Interesting. She jumped to a conclusion that's what he was going to do.

Andrew swept his arm to the porch. "We should go inside. Ken can wait in his room."

"We've already checked out and Eunice's turned it over already."

He glowered at her. "I'll be happy to pay Eunice for an additional night. I'm sure she won't mind then."

Wendy stumbled back and then straightened her shoulders, tipped her chin up. "Fine. Let's talk."

The sharp edge in her voice slithered out, akin to a rattlesnake giving a warning.

Wendy marched up the steps, Andrew behind her, and I was beside him. I nodded to Josie and Casey as we reached the porch. Ken stood in the doorway, his mouth thinning the instant he saw us.

"This doesn't look like a group of people about to enjoy home-baked cookies." He kept his words light, but the tone was hollow.

Wendy snapped. "You need to go upstairs until Andrew is ready to speak with you."

His eyes narrowed. "What's going on here? Wendy, do you want me to leave?"

She folded her arms over her chest and gave a small nod. "It's for the best. I'll be fine."

The hairs on the back of my neck prickled. Again, something in the way she spoke to Ken didn't sit right.

He took a menacing step toward Andrew. "She's been through a lot. Be nice to her."

Andrew arched a brow; his voice was like ice. "My brother was murdered. I'll be how I like."

Ken stalked up the stairs to the second floor, and after a door slammed, Andrew pointed to the sofa farthest from the windows. "We should sit."

Wendy took a spot at the end of the sofa, perched on the edge, folding her hands demurely in her lap.

Andrew sat on the chair near her. "Wendy, I want you to understand I'm not accusing you of anything, but I can't move forward with our wedding unless we're completely honest. I need truthful answers, and this is your chance to tell me everything."

Her eyes widened. "What are you talking about? We're getting married in eight weeks." She whimpered, "I thought you loved me."

"This isn't about love. This is about Rose Hill and Adam."

Confusion flickered over her face as she tilted her head. "I don't understand."

"You will." He shifted on the chair, his gaze fixed on her. "What's your relationship with Ken?"

"He's your cousin, so I'm nice to him. You know I helped him out with a small loan."

"How many loans?"

Wendy looked at her hands. "A few."

His eyes narrowed. "More than six figures?"

Her head snapped up, shock in her eyes and voice. "How do you know?"

He said dryly, "He's my cousin and I've bailed him out

more times than I care to admit. But what else is going on between you? Are you…involved?"

A deep flush spread across her cheeks. When she didn't answer the question, he said softly, "Just as I suspected."

"I love *you*, Andrew."

"That's why you met him in the park, hugging and kissing? Was it just the one time about a month ago? How often?"

She lifted her chin, defiant. "It's none of your business."

He pointed to the large diamond on her left hand. "That ring makes it my business."

Twisting the band nervously, she said, "Andrew…"

He held up his hand, cutting her off. "Stop. I need answers. Has he threatened you, either via text, email, or voicemail?"

"Maybe?" Her voice was so faint it was barely a whisper.

"Yes or no?"

I was surprised and impressed that Andrew was holding steady to his quest for the truth. Out of the corner of my eye, I noticed Casey slip into the room and stand near the check-in desk. Close enough to provide a police presence without causing a distraction.

She didn't answer him.

"All right. Moving on. You never said why you sent Josie Shaw the wrong crest for the invitations. You knew it would cause problems with my parents."

My gut flipped. He was going for the good stuff now.

Wendy slapped her hand on the arm of the sofa. "It was time to stop hiding the truth. It's not that big of a deal. If your father didn't want that piece of land, Ken would have gladly taken it off his hands."

Andrew leaned forward, and his voice was almost a growl. "And gamble that away, too? Is that why you told Ken about Rose Hill? The two of you came up with the scheme to get your hands on the land? I know you want to prove to the world that you're a shrewd realtor and should be the go-to person for commercial real estate. But killing Adam? Was Ken counting on the Posey inheritance to shift in his favor? Did he think that if you were successful in getting your hands on the land, you'd share it with him, and was the next step to kill me after the wedding for a large slice of the Posey fortune?"

He was repeating the same phrase over and over, *getting your hands on the land*. He was focused on Rose Hill, which might be better since he hadn't begun to deal with his grief for Adam.

"What are you talking about?" Her mouth formed a large O. "Do you think we killed Adam?"

"Where were you and Ken right before Adam was murdered? You weren't by my side as the future Mrs. Posey, that I know. It was only after Mom screamed his name that you appeared."

Clenching her fist, she shouted, "I was mingling with our guests!"

"And Ken?"

She jumped up, her breath coming in rapid bursts. "Stop this right now. I won't have you assassinate my character with Temperance and that cop in the room. I didn't kill Adam. But, yes, I told Ken about the crest and Rose Hill. Once he knew it was real and not just some family myth, he pressured me into helping him. He said he'd never breathe a word about my indiscretion."

Andrew snorted. "And you believed him?"

Her eyes flicked to the stairs. "Ask him. He'll confirm everything I'm saying."

"Or throw you under the bus." Andrew's response was merciless.

"He wouldn't do that," she whined.

I could hear the uncertainty in her words; this was the first crack in her facade.

"He's a gambler. Do you really think he has an honest

bone in his body? He was blackmailing you. Wendy, what would you have done to keep me in the dark?"

Dropping to her knees in front of his chair, she took his hands. "Andrew, I'm sorry for the stuff with Ken, but I promise I had nothing, absolutely nothing to do with Adam's death. I could never do something that heinous."

He eased his hands away. "And would you have married me after everything you've done to my family?"

"But Ken said…"

The words died on her lips as heavy footsteps thudded down the stairs.

With a slow mocking clap of his hands, Ken appeared, a smirk filled his lips, and a bit of humor danced in his eyes. "Excellent performance, Wendy." He focused on Andrew. "Cousin, if you want the real truth, you should ask me." He nodded to me and then to Casey, as his smirk widened. "Officer. Stick around. But don't bother with the handcuffs—you won't be needing them today." He tipped his head. "Or maybe you will."

20

———————

*E*unice burst through the door and stopped short once she crossed the threshold. Josie was hot on her heels.

"I deserve to know what's going on. This is my place of business, and if you—" Eunice jabbed a finger at Ken and then Wendy "have been up to no good, I deserve to know the truth."

Wendy got off the floor, eyes narrowing. "I'd be very careful if I were you, Eunice. You're not nearly as innocent as you pretend to be."

Color crept into the older woman's cheeks. "Well, you're an ungrateful woman. Andrew should walk out of here and not look back. The Poseys are the kindest people I've ever had the pleasure of knowing."

With arms crossed over her chest, Wendy cocked a hip and let out a snort. "Right. They've allowed you total access to the family's extensive library. You can borrow any book you want, any time you want. Isn't that right, Eunice?"

Wendy's razor-sharp words caused Eunice to step back as her hand flew to her mouth. *Why is Wendy taunting Eunice?* The tension between them crackled. One thing I knew for certain—there were more secrets than the Rose Hill silver mine. What exactly was Eunice hiding?

Ken cleared his throat. "Now, Wendy. We need to start at the beginning before you share all the interesting tidbits."

She gave him a sharp look. "Ken, maybe we shouldn't say anything without a lawyer."

He waved a dismissive hand. "We'll be fine, we haven't done anything wrong."

Andrew took a menacing step toward him. "Swindling your own family out of a valuable parcel of land to pay off gambling debts isn't a crime?"

"Who said anything about swindling? For the record, I am currently out of debt thanks to Wendy." He blew her a kiss. "You picked the perfect wife. Loyal to the family to a fault, and she's easy on the eyes, too."

Andrew lunged at Ken. I threw myself between them, pushing Andrew back. "Stop! This isn't helping."

He shrugged me off, his glare locked on Ken and Wendy. "Start talking, Cousin." The venom in his voice dripped with pain.

"Andrew." My voice sliced through the tension, drawing his attention to me. "Let me ask the questions."

Tension rolled off him in waves. He threw his hands up. "Fine."

I turned my attention to Wendy, Ken, and Eunice.

Casey and Josie were on the side of the room. Casey gave me a subtle nod. We were on the same page. She'd let me run with the questions while maintaining a strong police presence. With luck, I'd learn enough so she could arrest the killer.

"Ken, you allowed Wendy to bail you out with what exactly?"

He smirked. "Surely you can do better than that opener."

With the cocky attitude, I was liking him more and more for Adam's death. He was arrogant, slick, and driven by money. "Fine, then. Tell me how you and Wendy discovered the Posey family crest with the book and rose?"

He cocked a brow and gave an appreciative nod. "Going right to the heart of the puzzle. Impressive. After Wendy offered me a loan that Andrew refused, we began to talk. I joked that it was too bad Rose Hill wasn't a real gold mine, or should I say, a silver mine. Either way, it was money waiting for the right person."

"Initially, you believed it was a family legend."

He nodded. "If there was money—real money—to be made, Uncle Rob would have been eager to mine. Only now I've realized he has a bit of a do-gooder lurking inside his soul." He shrugged, "Who knew. It wasn't a trait *I* inherited." His self-satisfied grin spread. "I'm the black sheep of the family. Just ask my mother. As much as she's tried to *fix* me, it never took. I'm a lost cause."

He didn't seem unhappy; instead, it seemed he relished the title.

"What changed?" I glanced at Wendy. She had sunk into a chair, curling her shoulders in as if she wanted to disappear.

"When did you learn about the altered crest and dive into the secret?"

His grin widened. "I can't take credit for that. When Wendy was planning the engagement party and Andrew bailed on their meeting with Eunice, I volunteered to ride along. She joked it was too bad Rose Hill was just a story. That only reinforced my thoughts, like, why couldn't I have inherited something like *that* from my grandfather instead of a measly lump sum of cash? We were walking around the grounds of the inn and chatting, casually, when Eunice over-heard us."

Wendy's voice wavered. "That's when Eunice mentioned a book she'd read in the family library. Well, she didn't read it as much as memorize every detail. It described Rose Hill and the riches waiting to be discovered."

I whirled around to face Eunice. "You discovered the crest?"

She threw up her hands, exasperated. "In my defense, how was I supposed to know these two fortune hunters would kill Adam over it?"

Ken shook his hand as color slipped from his face.

Wendy shrieked. "What? Kill Adam? Neither Ken nor I killed him!"

Ken's jaw clenched. "I may be a lot of things, but a murderer isn't one of them." He turned to Andrew, his face pinched. "Do you really believe I could have killed him? We grew up together; I couldn't hurt him any more than I could you."

Andrew's silence and the hurt in his eyes were gut-wrenching. His gaze slid from Wendy to Ken to Eunice. "You'd cozy up to my fiancée, manipulate her into helping you get your slimy hands on the land, and you expect me to believe that you didn't attack Adam. Did you argue, and things got heated? Without thinking about the consequences, you struck him with that brick. Not meaning for it to be fatal, but it was."

"Andrew, I swear to you, I didn't attack Adam." For the first time, his voice shook and I saw sincerity flicker in Ken's eyes.

Andrew's unrelenting glare turned on Wendy. "Then it was you."

"No!" she cried, panic lacing her words. "I'd never hurt your brother."

I reached out, catching his arm. "It couldn't be Wendy, she's not tall enough to have struck him unless she was standing on a ladder."

"Then if we take Ken at his word and it's not physically possible for Wendy, who else..." his words faded as he looked at Eunice. "Who else was at the inn on Saturday? Who could Adam have encountered?"

"No one." Eunice's voice was calm—almost too calm.

"Eunice," I kept my tone neutral, "do you always wear a logo shirt?"

She sniffed and smoothed her hand over her crisp white shirt and khaki shorts. "If the inn is open, I'm in uniform."

I asked, "Do you have extras on hand in case you get dirty?"

"Of course I do."

My tone sharpened. "How many people work at the inn full-time?"

"Only me," Eunice stated. "I've fallen into a bit of a slump, so I only use contracted help."

"Like the kitchen helper?" I pressed. "Was it a lie when you said your helper quit on Thursday and you hadn't had time to replace her?"

She lifted her chin; defiance glinted in her eyes. "Is that any of your business?"

"It is—if you're guilty of murder."

Wendy sucked in a breath and stumbled back. Ken put out a steady hand to keep her from falling. Andrew advanced on Eunice, fury turning his blue-green eyes to ice.

My mouth went dry. I had been so focused on Wendy and Ken that I hadn't noticed all the little things that now screamed of her guilt. The shirt, the helper, the access. "Did you kill Adam?" I demanded.

Eunice's gaze darted around the room. "Adam wasn't *meant* to be the victim, it was…an accident."

The door banged open. Cissy yelled, "*You!*" Her voice cracked the air like a whip.

Eunice spun around. "Cissy, it's not what you think. I didn't intend for Adam to get hurt. You have to understand, I only meant to drum up business for the inn. Picture this: a future groom dies under mysterious circumstances. A member of the Posey family, his fiancée, is charged and convicted of the crime. This inn would be *the* ghoul seeker's holy grail. Think of what that would have done for the inn."

Casey asked, "You meant to kill Andrew and frame Wendy for the crime?"

"Yes." Eunice's eyes gleamed with twisted pride. "The idea of a quiet country inn becoming the infamous location where Andrew Posey died? It was the perfect way to grow my business. When I realized it was Adam, it was even better. He's known around the globe for his art. His death would bring me advertising I couldn't buy."

Cissy's fists clenched at her side as she approached. Rob was right behind her. "You killed my son—for profit? What's next, Eunice? Did you plan to kill Andrew, too, and then me and Rob to really enhance the inn's image as the place where the Posey family met their untimely death? That would be *great* for business." Her voice had reached a terrifying pitch.

"Of course not." Her voice cracked, "I'd never hurt you or Rob. You've been the closest thing that I've had to a family since Fred died."

Even as she spoke, she slowly inched closer to the swinging kitchen door.

"Stop right there, Eunice." Casey ordered, "I'm placing you under arrest for the murder of Adam Posey."

Crocodile tears rolled down Eunice's cheeks. "I'm sorry, Cissy." She shoved Casey into Wendy and Ken and bolted to the door. I sprang into action, tackling her as her fingers grazed the wood.

We tumbled across the floor as she clawed at my face. "Leave me alone!"

"Not this time, Eunice. You're finished."

My hand clamped onto her upper arm as I got up from the floor. Casey grabbed her other arm, snapping handcuffs in place.

Ken murmured, "I guess you needed them after all."

Casey flashed him an annoyed look and marched Eunice

to the front door. Officer Booker waited on the other side of the archway.

I said, "Stop."

Casey paused, glancing over her shoulder.

I met Eunice's wild-eyed stare. "You mentioned Oak Hollow Hideaway Inn, and the town's image was everything to you. But you didn't care that sordid scheme put a blight on everything."

"Image is what you make of it. Good or bad," Eunice said bitterly. "I wanted my business to thrive and all of you—" her gaze roamed the Posey family "you thought I was the sweet innkeeper who loved to read. That's why my plan would have worked. You've overlooked me for years. If it hadn't been for Temperance and Josie meddling, the evidence I planted in Ken and Wendy's suitcases would have sealed their fate."

"What made you attack Adam while the party was in full swing?" Josie asked.

Her lips curled into a sneer. "His photos. They were the story I couldn't control. He'd spent the day not just taking pictures of the party but of the entire property. He found my checklist. Notes on what I needed to do to blackmail those two. Stupidly, I left it next to the chair out back." Her voice dropped and she muttered, "I never should've agreed he could wander the property. It was careless."

I sucked in a sharp breath. "Eunice. Are you saying…"

Her eyes flashed as she glared at me. "I saw him taking pictures of my list. I begged him not to, but he said Andrew needed to be told about Wendy's plans for Rose Hill. He had to be stopped—so, I hit him. I didn't expect it to be fatal." Her words were flat, almost callous.

Cissy's mouth gaped open. Rob slid his arm around her waist as her knees buckled, guiding her to a bench.

Casey's tone was granite. "Eunice Moss, you're under

arrest for the murder of Adam Posey. Anything you say can be used against you."

"What will happen to my beautiful inn?" She lurched toward Rob, fear bled into her words. "Please, save my business."

His face contorted with rage and grief. "Save your inn? After you murdered my son?" Rising to his feet, his voice shook. "The last thing I'd ever do is help you." He turned his back on her and wrapped his arms around Cissy.

Casey's phone pinged. She looked at the screen. "Officer Booker, please escort Mrs. Moss to the station for processing. I'll be in shortly."

Booker guided Eunice from the inn to the waiting police car.

After closing the door, Casey pocketed her phone and knelt beside Cissy and Rob. "I just got a text from Pad Stone. He developed the black and white film and asked if we'd meet him at the station." She looked at Andrew. "He specifically asked for you and your parents to come."

Wendy took an unsteady step closer to Andrew. "What about me? I'm about to be part of the family." She paused. "Honey?"

He held out his right hand, and hesitantly, she placed her left in it. He twisted her engagement ring off. "I put this ring on your finger when I welcomed you into my life—and my family. I'm taking it back. You're a part of my past."

He gave Ken a weary gaze. "You're welcome to her. And for the record, even in my father's deepest haze of grief, he'd never have agreed to sign Rose Hill over to you. And if I have anything to say about it, you'll never darken our doorway again. Family doesn't destroy family."

Wendy grabbed his arm, her voice choked with pain. "Andrew. Wait. Can I make this up to you? You're the love of my life."

He peeled her fingers from his arm and pulled away. "I

feel sorry for you. *Money* is the love of your life. I was just a means to an end." He helped Cissy to her feet. "Mom. Dad. Let's go. I'm done here."

AFTER CASEY LEFT THE INN, Andrew and his parents followed her. Josie and I drove in silence. The road to the station felt endless. For the first few minutes, my brain churned with all that we had discovered from Ken, Wendy, and Eunice.

Finally, I said, "Josie, how could three people be so consumed by greed?"

She shook her head. "It's not like Wendy and Ken were directly responsible for Adam's death, but you're right. Ken's actions allowed Eunice to manipulate them, turning blackmail into an option. Wendy's ambition played right into her hands. Then Adam stumbled onto the list..." Josie released a stuttered exhale. "The entire situation is heartbreaking."

"Do you think Adam took pictures of incriminating evidence besides the note?" I asked quietly.

She looked at me. "We'll know soon enough. There is one thing I know: this will be excruciating for Cissy, Rob, and Andrew."

"And we'll be there to support them in any way that they need." Solving a case for people I knew was satisfying and heartbreaking.

Six months later...

I REACHED DOWN and scratched Hank's velvety soft ears. Josie sat at the kitchen table holding a creamy yellow envelope in her hands. An identical one lay on the table. The current family crest was engraved into the back with the words...

Veritas sub rosa. Truth beneath the rose.

She slit hers open, and a slow smile spread across her face. "It's an invitation for a private showing of Adam Posey's last photos to be held at the Oak Hollow Hideaway Inn."

I smiled back. "It's fitting that Rob and Cissy bought the inn and closed it to the public. No curiosity seekers will ever fulfill Eunice Moss's plan."

She read aloud. "Arrangements for the exhibition are credited to Padraic Stone, Eleanor McKenna Stone, and Andrew Posey."

"It'll be a perfect tribute to Adam's legacy," I said softly as I picked up Hank and held him close. "Did I tell you Cissy specifically asked for walnut brownies to be featured on the dessert trays?"

"Adam's favorite." Josie's eyes glistened as she smiled. "You know, this case wasn't as clean cut as the others, but I'm glad we were able to help put the guilty person behind bars and save Andrew from marrying a gold-digging opportunist."

I nodded, blinking away bittersweet tears. "Hopefully, this is the last time Casey needs us to investigate murder."

Are you ready to read more from Temperance and the gang in Oak Hollow?
Book 4 will release in November 2026

Keep reading for a sneak peek of
Books & Bribes
A Paranormal Witch Cozy Mystery
A Bookstore Cozy Mystery Series
Order Now
Or
Shop at Lucinda Race

Lucinda

A BOOK STORE COZY MYSTERY
Book One
Books & Bribes
LUCINDA RACE

BOOKS & BRIBES

CHAPTER 1

Lily

Achoo. A thick cloud of dust flew up from the pages of the hefty book that had fallen off the shelf. It barely missed my head as it hit the floor with a *thump.* I stumbled backward over a small stool and let out a scream as I tried desperately to catch myself on anything before falling.

A sandpaper-like feel scraped over my cheek from the wooden floor and I slowly opened my eyes. There was Milo, my gray tabby cat, hovering over me. I scratched his long, soft coat. "Hey, little man. I'm okay. Just took a tumble." I eased myself to a sitting position and gently rubbed the back of my head where it had connected with the floor. Not a great way to end a Monday.

A deep gravelly voice said, "You've been lying there for several minutes out cold. I didn't think you'd ever wake up."

I looked around. "Who's there?" My heart rate increased as I scrambled to my feet and grabbed the heavy book. As I hurried down the aisle of the bookshop, scanning right and left, I wondered who was in my store. I was certain I'd locked the front door at four on the dot after my last customer left.

I checked the empty sitting area in front of the oversized north-facing windows. It comprised of two wingback chairs, a small table between them, and a round table in front of them. It was great natural light for reading. But I was alone.

Shaking my head gingerly, I surmised it must be the residual effect from hitting my head. Glancing at the fat blue book in my hand, *Practical Beginnings,* I decided I'd climb the stepstool tomorrow and find a place for it. Walking back to the wide wooden counter, I dropped it on top and stroked Milo's soft fur. "Ready to go home?" My besties were meeting me at the library for classic movie night. Tonight was *Death on the Nile* by Agatha Christie, and I didn't want to be late.

I had locked the cash register when I heard a scratchy, but kind voice say, "Ready when you are."

With the stapler in my hand, I twirled around, shaking it in the air. "I demand you show yourself!"

"Lily, it's me. Your old buddy Milo."

"Stop it. Right now!" Who was in my shop?

"Look at your cat," the voice urged.

My heart thudded in my chest. Was something wrong with my sweet baby? "Milo?" I scooped him into my arms and held him tight.

"Need. To. Breathe." He squirmed in my arms and escaped to the counter.

I stumbled back against a long table stacked with bestsellers. Some dropped to the floor as my weight sagged against it. "Did you just speak?" The words came out as a croak.

"I've been waiting for you to open that book for ages. Remember Aunt Mimi asked you to read it on your last birthday?"

I nodded, dumbfounded. This couldn't be happening. I could hear him, but his tiny mouth wasn't moving. I lifted my hand and grazed the slight bump on the back of my head. My cat was talking to me. Wait, I must have hit my head harder than I thought or worse, had something possessed me? I rubbed the back of my head again. Ouch. "No, I must be concussed."

I walked around the room, checking to make sure the windows were secured and double-checked the front door was locked. "Yup, all tight as a drum."

"We already knew that." Once again, it was the same voice. My legs jiggled like rubber. I dropped to the chair and put my head between my legs just in case I felt faint. After a few seconds, I sat up. This was stupid. I was having a conversation with a prankster.

"Milo, if you're really talking, come over here and sit in this other chair."

I watched as he walked to the edge of the counter and dropped to the floor, only to hop up in the chair opposite me. This couldn't be happening. No way he understood.

Licking his front paw and rubbing it above his eye, he said, "Now what do you need me to do for my next parlor trick so that you'll believe me?"

"Tell me what I'm thinking?" I leaned closer, giving him full access to my face. The close proximity would help me see if his mouth was moving.

"I'm not telepathic. I'm your familiar and yes, that means you're a witch. Finally, the truth is out." He stretched over the cushion and rolled on his back as if I was supposed to scratch his tummy. "Feel free."

Like when Milo always rolled over, I obliged by scratching his belly and his eyes would close in contentment, but this time he was giving me directions where I should be scratching.

"If you're going to be bossy, I'm done." I went to stand up and dropped back in the chair. "Wait, what did you say about being a witch? I own a bookshop. There is nothing special about me."

My cat opened his eyes and he rolled to his side, never

bothering to blink. "You can believe that's nothing special, but a few witches live in Pembroke Cove, and you are one of them."

Once again, I felt as if I had fallen from the stool and conked my head, but I was sitting on a comfy chair, talking with my cat who just announced I was a witch. "Wait." My thoughts were spinning. "Does that mean Aunt Mimi is one, too?"

"Stop repeating yourself, and now you're catching on." Milo jumped to the floor and looked up. "I thought you said we were going home. I'm hungry."

My breath came rapidly and my head swam. This couldn't be happening. I must be dreaming. As I bent over to put my head between my knees, which seemed to be the thing to do again, a tapping on the glass in the door drew my attention. Who on earth would stop by now? I looked at my watch. It was almost five. Again came the insistent knocking.

I got to my feet, albeit unsteadily, and waited until I felt I could plaster a smile on my face before going to the door. When I peeked out, relief washed over me and my breathing slowed. Why I was being such a nervous Nellie was beyond me. Must be all this talk of familiars and witches. With a glance over my shoulder, I jabbed a finger in Milo's direction. "Shush."

"No one else can hear me. When I talk, they hear a cute little meow coming from my tiny mouth."

I frowned. "Tiny is debatable at this point." I pulled open the door. The minute I saw his handsome face and the dreamy hazel eyes, my knees went weak. It was one of my oldest and dearest friends and also the guy I'd been in love with my entire life. Gage Erikson.

"Hi there. I was expecting to see you later at the library."

Gage walked in and looked around. "I thought I heard you talking. Are you alone?"

Heat flushed my cheeks. This wasn't something I was

about to share with anyone, having a conversation with a cat and he talked back. I forced a grin and added an extra dose of cheeriness to my voice. "Just talking to Milo. There's no one else here."

Gage bent over and scratched between the kitty's ears. Instead of a purr, I heard, "Hmm, that feels good. Thanks, Detective Cutie."

There was no reaction from the man, so at least there was that. Milo opened one eye and I would swear the cat winked at me.

"Gage, what brings you around? Did you want to drive to the movie together?" I clamped my mouth shut. That sounded way too much like a date and I didn't want to do anything to make our friendship awkward so I rushed ahead with, "Nikki and Steve are meeting us there and maybe even Aunt Mimi and Nate O'Brien."

"Sounds like it's going to be a packed house." He looked at me while he scooped up Milo to continue giving the kitty attention.

"I guess." Seeing Gage holding Milo was like kryptonite to me, causing my heart to do all kinds of crazy flips. Anyone who loved someone else's cat had to be a keeper, right? I sighed, and his brow quirked.

"You okay?"

"Oh. Yes. I fell off the stool earlier and hit my head."

Concern filled his golden-hazel eyes. He deposited Milo in the chair and took a step in my direction. "Where did you hit it?"

My hand went to the tender spot on the back. "I'm fine."

"Turn around so I can take a look."

I did as he asked, enjoying being fussed over a little, but not wanting to appear like some weak girl who needed his attention like those girls at the coffee shop. They were always giggling whenever he walked in, especially when he used to wear his police officer's uniform. He pushed ever so slightly on the spot that had connected with the floor and tears sprang to my eyes and I cried out, *"Ouch.* That hurts!"

His laugh was comforting. "Guess I found the spot. You should put ice on it and take it easy for tonight."

I turned back to face him. "I can't miss the movie. It's one of my favorites."

"Mine too, but that's why I stopped by. I can't make it tonight. I have to cover a shift for Mac Sullivan. His wife's gone into labor and we're short a man."

"That's exciting. About the new baby I mean, not about you working." I had to hold my disappointment in check again so as not to appear as anything more than a friend. "We'll miss having you there to chow down on popcorn and red licorice."

Gently he tucked a stray lock of my hair back behind my ear, a motion he had done thousands of times. But it made my heart race. I kept my eyes glued to the old oriental carpet in the middle of the room. No way was I going to let him see my eyes. He was way too perceptive and would see how I felt about him which I've spent years hiding.

"Maybe I'll swing by tomorrow around ten with coffee?"

When I looked into his eyes, I wondered if I saw a flicker of hope that I would say yes. Which I would, about anything. Dang it, in my head I sounded like a freshman in high school with a crush on the football star. "That'd be great. But if you're bringing coffee, any chance you can get one of those pecan buns, you know, with extra icing?"

"Is that your way of asking if I'll stop at The Sweet Spot?"

"Well, you offered coffee, and William makes the best pastries in three towns." I playfully batted my eyelashes just because I could and knew it always made him laugh.

Right on cue, he grinned. "That can be arranged." His cell rang, and he glanced at the screen. "I gotta take off. Duty calls."

He dropped an almost kiss on my cheek on his way out

the door and called over his shoulder, "See you in the morning." And then he was gone.

After a long sigh escaped my body, Milo said, "Really? Do you think he does not know that you're into him?"

Turning my back on him, I said, "I will not start talking to my cat about my love life."

Milo trotted in the direction to where I stored his cat carrier. "You mean your nonexistent love life, don't you?"

"Milo?" I meant for it to come out as a warning to hush up, but it sounded more like a question to my ears. "Do you think Gage knows I have a crush on him?"

"Yeah. And if you opened your eyes, you might see the feeling is mutual."

When I finally got to the library a little after six, the usual group had gathered in the community room to watch the film. My best friend Nikki was there with her boyfriend Steve, and my aunt was there with Nate. Marshall Stone was running the projector and Teddy Roberts and Jill Dilly were there too. The group was rounded out with a few teenagers from the high school and a couple of new faces. Typically, there'd be a few more stragglers before the film actually got started. This was shaping up to be a fun evening.

I waved to Meredith across the room, one of the librarians who worked there. She was a quiet woman, with a long blond braid down her back and round wire-rimmed glasses giving her a studious look. With a shy smile, she returned my wave and looked at her boss, the head librarian, Flora Gray. She was bustling about, making snide comments about how tomorrow, she'd be vacuuming up popcorn, candy wrappers, and heaven only knew what else from the floor. She was not a fan of movie night.

"Flora?" I stopped her as I helped set up the chairs. "Why don't you join us tonight? It's a classic Agatha Christie."

Her eyes narrowed and she glared at me. "I'm a librarian.

That fact should be enough to explain. I prefer books over any other form of entertainment. Especially when it's in black and white." She lifted her chin as disdain dripped from her words.

She didn't need to be so snarky. "I was trying to include you so you'd see what a wonderful group of people attend."

Meredith passed by, her arms loaded with books. "Flora, you know the movie buffs always leave the room immaculate. I don't think there is any need to be so harsh on Lily."

Flora gave Meredith a withering look, and she hurried to the other side of the library. Flora wiggled a large keyring in front of me. "I'll give this to your aunt, and she can lock up. But I'll be back later tonight to check on things. Everything had best be in place. And for once, clean up after yourselves." She pointed to the dish of hard candies on the side table. "Get rid of those. They draw ants."

I did not understand where she was coming from. Our group never left a mess. In fact, we cleaned the restrooms and the small kitchenette every month. It was odd she pointed out the candy dish since I did not know who brought it. But it didn't matter; the place would be spotless before we locked up. "Don't worry, Flora. I'll make sure everything is clean and tidy."

She jabbed a finger that almost touched my chest. "See that you do."

I watched the older woman march out of the room. Through the doorway I kept an eye on her just in case she came back for round two. Her short steel-gray hair was in a no-nonsense style. She always dressed exactly the same way. A starched white blouse, a horsehead broach, and black slacks with sturdy tie shoes. In the winter, she added a fisherman knit sweater to stave off the stiff ocean breeze as she biked from her home to the library. Even in the snow, she still biked. I could never figure out how, since the winds off the water were enough to push a car around, let alone a biker. I often thought she looked like the wicked witch from *The Wizard of Oz*, riding her bike in the tornado. But it was none of my business. At least I took comfort in knowing she treated everyone the same as me. She was an old biddy and thought she was doing the town a favor by letting groups hold events there.

At one time, Flora had tried to put an end to our gatherings. Even though she was on the board of elders, the rest of the group had intervened and reminded her it was a public space and community-minded groups could use it as long as it was posted to the schedule.

Pushing all thoughts aside, I turned my attention to Nikki, my best friend for life. We were complete opposites. She had long strawberry-blond hair while mine was dark in a pixie cut; her eyes were blue and mine, brown, and we always had each other's backs. She held up the DVD for Marshall to see.

As she grew closer and smiled at me, she asked, "What did the old bat complain about tonight?"

Marshall looked at us and said in his best Sherlock Holmes voice, "Fair to say, everything. I swear, how can someone as cantankerous as her even want to live in our fair town?"

Standing over six feet and strong as an ox, he owned and worked a vegetable farm on the outskirts of town. Years in the sun had left him with deep creases in his weatherworn face. Marshall had been running the projector for the last five years and, like everyone in Pembroke Cove it seemed, had at least one run-in with Flora. The last time she had been downright vicious when she thought he had broken the projector. It turned out all that was wrong was he had unplugged it at the end of the night.

People had taken their seats and the lights had just shut off when I heard Aunt Mimi scream, *"Help!* Somebody help!"

Keep reading for a sneak peek of
Books & Bribes

A Paranormal Witch Cozy Mystery
A Bookstore Cozy Mystery Series
Order Now
Or
Shop at Lucinda Race

Or if you've already read the first 12 books in this series, did you know book 13 is being released in August 2026?

Order today

Covens & Clues

REVIEWS & NEWSLETTER

If You Loved Walnut Brownies & Murder
Leave a Review
Reviews help other readers discover books they'll love—and
they mean the world to authors.
If you enjoyed this story, please consider leaving a review.
Even a short review makes a difference.
Bookbub:
Goodreads:
Amazon
Barnes and Noble
Kobo
Apple Books
Google Play

Stay Connected with Lucinda
Join my reader community and be the first to hear about:
New releases
Subscriber-only specials
Bonus content and sneak peeks
Early access to upcoming books

I hope you want to keep up with my crazy antics of writing, gardening, cooking, and life with the pup.

Not ready to stop reading yet? If you sign up for my newsletter at www.lucindarace.com/newsletter, you will receive Cookies & Capers as my thank-you gift for choosing to get my newsletter.

This novella is only available by signing up for my newsletter

📖 Sign Up Here:
https://lucindarace.com/newsletter/
Thank you for being part of this journey!
— Lucinda

COZY MYSTERY BOOKS

All ebooks and paperback copies can be ordered from my website at:
website at:
Shop at Lucinda Race

A Bookstore Cozy Mystery Series
Book 1 — Books & Bribes
Book 2 — Catnaps & Crimes
Book 3 — Tea & Trouble\
Book 4 — Scares & Dares
Book 5 — Holidays & Homicide
Book 6 — Leprechauns & Larceny
Book 7 - Magicians & Murder
Book 8 — Artifacts & Amulets
Book 9 — Cranberries & Criminals
Book 10— Broomsticks & Blooms
Book 11 Fishing & Forgery
Book 12 — Weddings & Wands
Book 13 — Covens & Clues

Dress Designer Cozy Mystery Series
Book 1 — Ghosts & Gowns

Book 2 — Buttons & Burglary
Book 3 — Pleats & Poison
Book 4 — Ribbons & Robbery

Temperance Matthews Cozy Mystery Series
Book 1 — Just Desserts & Murder
Book 2 — Cupcakes & Murder
Book 3 — Walnut Brownies & Murder
Book 4 - Coming Soon

Witches of Robins Pointe
A Paranormal Cozy Mystery Series
Inherited Magic & Murder 2027
Touch of Magic February 2027
Waiting for Magic March 2027

Visit Lucinda Online
Website: www.lucindarace.com
Join the Newsletter: https://lucindarace.com/newsletter/

ROMANCE BOOKS

**All ebooks and paperback copies can be ordered from my website at:
Shop at Lucinda Race**

Small-Town Romance
The Price Family Romance Series
Book 1 — Breathe
Book 2 — Crush
Book 3 — Blush
Book 4 — Vintage
Book 5 — Bouquet
Book 6 — *Cantina* November 2026
Price Family Romance Boxset

The McKenna Family Romance Series
Book 1 — Lost and Found
Love never ends... A widow who talks to her husband's ghost and her handsome single neighbor who has secretly loved her for years.
Book 2 — The Journey Home
Book 3 — The Last First Kiss
Book 4 — Ready to Soar

Book 5 — Love in the Looking Glass
Book 6 — Magic in the Rain
Book 7 — After All These Years
McKenna Family Romance Boxset

The MacLellan Sisters Romance Series
Book 1 — Old and New
Book 2 — Borrowed
Book 3 — Blue
MacLellan Sisters Trilogy

Cowboys of River Junction
Contemporary Western Cowboy Romance Series
Book 1 — Second Chances in Montana
Book 2 — Stars Over Montana
Book - 3 Hiding in Montana
Book - 4 Moonlight Over Montana
Cowboys of River Junction Boxset

Sunsets of New England Romance Series
Book 1 — The Matchmaker and The Marine
Book 2 — Shamrocks Are A Girl's Best Friend
Book - 3 Love, Weddings & Second Chances - A Collection
Book - 4 Holiday Hearts - A Collection
Book - 5 Holly Berries & Hockey Pucks
Book - 6 A Secret Santa Christmas

ABOUT THE AUTHOR

Award-winning and best-selling author Lucinda Race has been captivated by stories for as long as she can remember. A lifelong reader who fell head over heels for cozy mysteries and heartfelt romances as a young girl, she now brings that same magic to her own books.

Stories Filled with Heart, Hope, and a Hint of Mystery
Although her writing career began in nonfiction, storytelling always called her back home. Today, she delights readers with the beloved McKenna Family Romance series and the Paranormal Cozy Nook Bookstore Series—creating charming small towns, lovable characters, and page-turning mysteries filled with heart.

Whether crafting a swoon-worthy romance or a twisty cozy mystery, Lucinda writes the kinds of stories she loves to read —stories that leave readers smiling long after the final page.

Now with over 40 books published, she's living her dream and loves connecting with readers at LucindaRace.com.

SOCIAL MEDIA

Follow Me on Social Media

Like my Facebook page
Join Lucinda's Heart Racer's Reader Group on Facebook
Twitter @lucindarace
Instagram @lucindaraceauthor
BookBub
Goodreads
Pinterest
YouTube

www.ingramcontent.com/pod-product-compliance
Lightning Source LLC
Chambersburg PA
CBHW050659070726

47595CB00014B/552